OF
ONE BLOOD
Or, The Hidden Self

OF ONE BLOOD

Or, The Hidden Self

PAULINE HOPKINS

Introduction by Deborah E. McDowell

WSP

WASHINGTON SQUARE PRESS
New York London Toronto Sydney

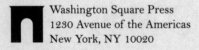 Washington Square Press
1230 Avenue of the Americas
New York, NY 10020

ISBN: 0-7434-6769-8

First Washington Square Press trade paperback edition February 2004

10 9 8 7 6 5 4 3 2 1

Manufactured in the United States of America

For information regarding special discounts for bulk purchases,
please contact Simon & Schuster Special Sales at 1-800-456-6798
or business@simonandschuster.com

Originally published serially in 1902-03 by *Colored American Magazine*

INTRODUCTION

As Pauline Hopkins's *Of One Blood* hurtles toward its fantastical ending, the narrator exclaims once more the premise of the novel's title:

> The slogan of the hour is "keep the Negro down!" but who is clear enough in vision to decide who hath black blood and who hath it not? Can any one tell? No, not one; for in His own mysterious way He has united the white race and the black race in this new continent.

To lend authority and reinforcement to the claim, the narrator summons scripture—"Of one blood I made all nations of man to dwell upon the whole face of the earth" (Acts 17:26)— then handily concludes, "No man can draw the dividing line between the two races, for they are both of one blood!"

The two races are, of course, black and white, and the "dividing line" between them is the "color line," which W. E. B. Du Bois famously coined "the problem of the twentieth century" in *The Souls of Black Folk* (1903). That same year, *Of One Blood*, which had begun serialization in 1902, appeared in its final installment in *The Colored American Magazine*, ending a remarkably prolific period for Hopkins in fiction writing. It began in 1900 with "The Mystery Within Us" (widely considered the germ for *Of One Blood*), a short story published in the inaugural issue of *The Colored American Magazine. Contending Forces: A Romance Illustrative of Negro Life North and South*, the first and arguably most well known of Hopkins's novels, was also published in 1900, followed in close succession by *Hagar's Daughter; A Story of Southern Caste Prejudice* (written under the pseudonym "Sarah A. Allen," her mother's maiden name) and serialized between 1901 and 1902. Next came *Winona: A Tale of Negro Life in the South and Southwest* (1902–03). That these works appeared so closely on the heels of the other, each betraying the signs of hasty composition, attests to the urgency on Hopkins's part to make her mark in the literary world, although her ambitions were not merely limited to the novel. She published short stories, essays, biographical sketches, feature articles, and a history primer, all in the short five-year span between 1900 and 1905, during part of which time she served as literary editor of *The Colored American Magazine*. Undoubtedly she meant to make an impact on the wider realm of arts and letters.

Born in Portland, Maine, in 1859, Hopkins, who grew up in Boston and was educated in the city's public schools, began her artistic career as a playwright, actress, and performer, mainly with the Hopkins Coloured Troubadors, a theatrical troupe, which included family members, who gave concerts throughout the Boston area. While scholars are still piecing together the details of the early phases of Hopkins's career, they have uncovered some of her plays, including *The Slave's Escape; or the Underground Railroad*, produced in 1880, and at least one full-length biography is under way.

When Hopkins resumed her publishing career in 1900, she was entering a new phase of her career, which coincided with an auspicious era in African-American literary production. The turn of the century witnessed an efflorescence of black literary talent—including Charles Chesnutt, Paul Laurence Dunbar, Anna Julia Cooper, Sutton Griggs, to name only the most prominent—who, as Richard Yarborough notes, found more "outlets for publication open to them than had been afforded to blacks at any time since the height of the abolition movement." Not only did their work appear in such leading white periodicals as *Harper's Magazine*, *Century Magazine*, and *Atlantic Monthly*, adds Yarborough, the simultaneous "rise of Afro-American journals provided these writers alternative, often less restrictive forums for expression" (xxvii-xxviii). *The Colored American Magazine* was one such journal, and Hopkins was a driving creative force behind it, serving as its literary editor from 1903 to 1904, when the magazine changed hands. Now backed financially by Booker T. Washington, whose policies and politics Hopkins had openly critiqued, the magazine was no longer a viable platform for the expression of her political ideas and literary ambitions.

Hopkins and her original cohorts had hoped the *Colored American Magazine* would function as a forum for advancing the "interest of blacks" and promoting the "development of Afro-American art and literature," as its mission statement read. Like most of her black contemporaries, she believed that literature, fiction especially, had transformative social value and counter-discursive power. As she put the matter in her preface to *Contending Forces*, "Fiction is of great value to any people as a preserver of manners and customs—religious, political, and social. It is a record of growth and development from generation to generation." Then, striking a characteristically hortatory note, she continued:

No one will do this for us; we must ourselves develop

the men and women who will faithfully portray the inmost thought and feelings of the Negro with all the fire and romance which lie dormant in our history, *and as yet unrecognized by writers of the Anglo-Saxon Race* [emphasis in text].

Although Hopkins stopped short of naming any of these "writers of the Anglo-Saxon Race," likely candidates abounded. At one extreme her list would certainly have included Thomas Dixon, whose rabidly racist novels *The Leopard's Spots* (1901) and *The Clansman* (1903), the latter the inspiration for D. W. Griffith's *Birth of a Nation*, were prototypical of nineteenth-century hysteria about race, nationality, and miscegenation. Such hysteria converged in one of the most virulent stereotypes in popular American literature: the ever-threatening image of the black male beast/rapist always at the ready to violate white southern womanhood and pollute the purity of the Anglo-Saxon bloodstream. But Hopkins might also have had less extremist writers in mind, such as William Dean Howells, the distinguished editor of *The Atlantic Monthly* who regularly published the work of black writers, including the early essays of W. E. B. Du Bois, and championed the poetic talents of Paul Laurence Dunbar. However, in such works as his novella *An Imperative Duty* (1892), Howells seemed to contribute his own share to the store of irrational ideas about percentages and rations of black blood to white circulating wildly in nineteenth-century popular discourse and racist pseudoscience.

In titling her novel *Of One Blood*, Hopkins can be said to have entered the lists to contest these cultural fictions concerning race and blood, the reinforcements, as it were, propping up the color line and maintaining white supremacy. Hopkins understood, of course, that the "color line," the invisible but powerful social divide structured to "separate" the races, was so fiercely guarded and so violently policed in turn-of-the-century U.S. even as (undoubtedly because) crossing it had mainly proved the custom of the country. Otherwise, the need would never have arisen for the "one drop rule" or any other fiction of "black" blood, measured in quarters, eighths, sixteenths, and such. Nor would there have been a need to catalogue the "foolproof" signs of blackness—purplish scrotums, dark half-moons at the fingernail beds, the dusky outer rims of the ear, coarser hair at the nape of the neck—all supposedly detectable markers even when the face read "white." While it could certainly be assumed that Hopkins was well schooled in these and other occult details of racial myth and folklore, her concerns in *Of One Blood* lie primarily in exposing and unraveling the entangled genealogies of blacks and whites, the irrefutable evidence that they were literally, biologically, "of one blood."

*   *   *   *   *

A largely self-educated intellectual, Pauline Hopkins had clearly absorbed, though not uncritically, the nineteenth-century obsession with the roots of mankind, with taxonomies of "difference" classifying individuals, nations, and "races" according to a set of immutably "distinguishing" traits and spiritual types. This obsession with racial "difference," some of it derived from German romanticism, seized the U.S. cultural imagination precisely at the moment when the slavery controversy was at its boiling point and the amateur "science" of ethnology was on the rise.

In its heyday during the 1840s and 1850s, the American school of ethnology was associated with a few influential figures: Samuel G. Morton, Josiah Nott, George Gliddon, and the famed naturalist Louis Agassiz, all proponents of "polygenicism," the idea that the roots of humankind lay not in one (monogenesis) but several (polygenesis) creations. This emphasis on separate creations, on the inviolable distinctions among members of the "human family," posed a challenge, as Reginald Horsman writes, "both to a religion which viewed mankind as descended from common ancestors and to a science, at least since Darwin," which "classified human beings as belonging to one species with one set of innate characteristics, albeit hierarchically related." It was obviously not an accident, Stephen Jay Gould suggests, that "a nation still practicing slavery and expelling its aboriginal inhabitants from their home lands should have provided a base of theories that blacks and Indians [were] separate species, inferior to whites" (93), nor that such theories, I would add, would be certified as scientific truth.

In setting her novel first in Boston, Hopkins closed in on one of the nerve centers of the U.S. cultural debate on "blood," bloodlines, and the roots of the "human family": Harvard University, from which perch Louis Agassiz became one of the leading spokesmen for polygenesis. This is clearly not the space for a thoroughgoing treatment of Agassiz's ideas or research methods, but scholars have argued—Stephen Jay Gould most forcefully—that Agassiz's ideas about separate species were clearly colored by his actual interactions with black Americans, evidenced in letters he wrote soon after immigrating to the U.S. and assuming his post at Harvard. Translated by Gould, these letters, expurgated not surprisingly from the "official" collection of Agassiz's correspondence, cut to the quick of his ideas about bloodlines. In a letter to his mother about an encounter with blacks in a Philadelphia hotel, he writes, "It is impossible for me to repress the feeling that they are not of the same blood as us" (Gould, 95).

In subsequent letters, some written in the midst of the Civil War, Agassiz expressed his doubts concerning the role of blacks in a reunited nation, especially given the threat of miscegenation:

> *Conceive for a moment the difference it would make in future ages, for the prospect of republican institutions and our civilization generally, if instead of the manly population descended from cognate nations the United States should hereafter be inhabited by the effeminate progeny of mixed races, half Indian, half Negro, sprinkled with white blood . . . How shall we eradicate the stigma of a lower race when its blood has once been allowed to flow freely into that of our children?* (Gould, 98–99)

Of course, by this point in American history, the blood of the "cognate nations" had already been flowing freely with that of the "lower races," which idea Hopkins sought to establish in *Of One Blood*. Indeed, the argument, propounded throughout the narrative in various guises, is that the blood has flown so freely between the races that any attempt to sort and separate them was inevitably confounded. That Reuel, Dianthe, and Aubrey are all ultimately revealed to be children of both the same father *and* mother—the one "white," the other "black"—establishes their "kinship" in a single racial "family." Hopkins reinforces these scenes of recovered origins and family reunion, common in the literature of the era, with an equally familiar changeling trope famously dramatized in such novels as Mark Twain's *Pudd'nhead Wilson*. If a "black" baby could be switched at birth and made "white," as happens to Hopkins's Aubrey Livingston, or if a "black" could pass for "white," as does her Reuel Briggs, then racial distinctions were founded on flimsy and artificial signs indeed, on what Twain termed "fiction[s] of law and custom." Thus the narrator's question in *Of One*

Blood—"Who is clear enough in vision to decide who hath black blood and who hath it not?"—posed an implicit challenge to the visual logics on which biological understandings of race depended, particularly the "one drop rule" that made ancestry the unimpeachable determinant of "blackness."

In her attempt to sidestep such ocular logics and demystify biological definitions of race, Hopkins turned to what was then being called "the new psychology," even though this may have seemed an unlikely base from which to mount a challenge to racist conceptions of African-American identity, for, as Terry Otten observes, the psychological literature of the day, especially that published in academic journals, often colluded in producing such conceptions. But as Otten goes on to say, turn-of-the-century psychology was far from being a coherent academic discipline. Hopkins turned the discipline's incoherence to her own advantage, finding in William James a useful ally. James was known to combine aspects of the emergent field of academic psychology with various forms of popular psychology—mesmerism, spiritualism, mysticism, and mind-cure (or Christian Science)—which were much the rage in late-nineteenth- and early-twentieth-century middle- and upper-class society. Boston seemed a magnet for such spiritual "sciences" and philosophies which James's brother, Henry, had mined for his novel *The Bostonians*.

Of One Blood opens with a bold appropriation of William James, albeit in disguise. Reuel, Hopkins's protagonist, a physician with a specialty in mesmerism, pores over "The Unclassified Residuum," identified as a work "eagerly sought by students of mysticism and dealing with the great field of new discoveries in psychology" (442). As several scholars have noted, however, the passages Reuel is reading come not from Alfred Binet, Hopkins's fictive attribution, but from "The

Hidden Self," a review essay which James published in *Scribner's Magazine* (1890) and later reworked for inclusion in his collection *The Will to Believe*.

A founding member of the American branch of the Society for Psychical Research, James sympathized in "The Hidden Self" with radical notions about the nature of the unconscious. As Cynthia Schrager notes, James "maintained a receptivity to the irrational and nonmaterial" realm and to phenomena which transcended what "science" could see, even though many of his academic colleagues greeted such ideas with great skepticism (Schrager, 183).

In selecting "The Hidden Self" as subtitle, Hopkins settled on a trope as protean and elastic as the book's twin metaphor of blood. I agree with Schrager that Hopkins translates the "notion of a hidden self from the intrapsychic field . . . to the social field." For example, Schrager suggests, in the figure of Aubrey Livingston, Hopkins exposes the "hidden self at the foundation of Anglo-American subjectivity and the suppression of the truth of miscegenation upon which the color line depends." She adds, the "hidden self" serves Hopkins simultaneously as a "metaphor for the suppressed history of oppressive social and familial relations under the institution of slavery" (196). But I would add that, these material realities notwithstanding, Hopkins is equally invested in the intrapsychic, intraracial implications of the "hidden self," sharing with her contemporary W. E. B. Du Bois a belief in "the souls of black folk," however nebulously defined the concept of "soul" remained both in his work and hers. In other words, the "hidden self" might be regarded as the conceptual equivalent of Du Bois's "soul." Both deliberately elevated psyche over soma, mind over body, spirit over matter, in definitions of race. Reuel's imaginary mystical text, "The Unclassified Residuum," could also be read as a hidden reference to the residue that ethnology, its sights riveted on blood fractions and the body, had left "unclassified."

That Hopkins attributed the fictive "Unclassified Residuum" to Binet was surely not accidental, for his work *On Double Consciousness* was one of many likely sources of Du Bois's signature formulation "double consciousness." While the idea of a double or split self arose in the literature of the romantic period, "double consciousness" acquired popularity primarily as a psychiatric disorder describing a condition whereby two distinctive personalities inhabited the same body, each independent of the other. Du Bois reformulated the medical meaning of "double consciousness," transforming it from a pathological to a privileged condition, characterized by "second sight." Long a champion of Du Bois, Hopkins created more than one fictional character clearly modeled on him: Will Smith from *Contending Forces* and most obviously Reuel from *Of One Blood*, who is gifted with "the power of second sight."

Hopkins shared with Du Bois the urge to mine the new psychology for the elements of a "new psychology" for African-Americans as well as a new "race" concept. This new psychology would seemingly be grounded in the mystical/spiritual realm, even though that was the realm to which nineteenth-century pseudoscientific racialism (and racism) had already relegated blacks. Or, as Cynthia Schrager puts it, while the Jamesian figure of the "hidden self" made "inroads against the determinism of turn-of-the-century racial constructions of self," it risked relegating African-Americans to the role of the "repressed unconscious" of the Anglo-American, as well as to the zone of the "irrational." This was a risk Hopkins was prepared to take, and in this she was not alone. In the interest of squaring off against ethnological ideas of Anglo-Saxon "purity" and supremacy over "primitive" races, Hopkins, along with many of her contemporaries, claimed "racial difference" for alternative ends and aims, namely to resurrect an obscured African past the supposed glory of which would restore a damaged collective African-American consciousness. Over and against the idea of a glorious Anglo-Saxon civilization threatened with "mongrelization" and ultimate extinction by racial intermixture Hopkins sets an equally glorious African civilization that predated Anglo-Saxonism by centuries.

Of One Blood's "back-to-Africa" plot, as some have termed it, has consistently baffled critics, who have trouble reconciling the monogenetic implications of that title with the polygenetic implications of "the hidden self" of its subtitle. If we are all "of one blood," critics ask, how can the novel logically conclude, as it does, with a recuperation of distinct bloodlines, one the source of an "originary" African identity, existing in its own state of imaginary purity before Anglo-Saxon contamination, before the implantation of racist and racialist fantasies into the U.S. cultural imagination.

While Hopkins is clearly critical of racist pseudo-science, her goal in *Of One Blood* is clearly not to abandon race thinking entirely. As a devotee of W. E. B. Du Bois, Hopkins was rather more inclined to devise a usable conception of race such as Du Bois attempted to outline in such controversial essays as "The Conservation of Races" (1897) and "The Concept of Race" (1940). In the former, first presented as an address to the American Negro Academy, he defined race as a "vast family of human beings, generally of common blood and language, always of common history, traditions, and impulses, who are both voluntarily and involuntarily striving together for the accomplishment of certain more or less vividly conceived ideals of life" (Gates, 177–78). Contemporary scholars have exhaustively critiqued Du Bois's ideas about race, but they enjoyed some currecy among many of those African-American intellectuals who classed themselves "race men" and "race women" at the turn of the centruy. For them "blood" was that which bound them together at a moment when a decidedly different meaning of the same threatened them with the violence of caste and circumscription, at best, and the noose of the lyncher's rope, at worst.

*   *   *   *   *

Given these realities, one is justified in asking, why fit a tale of genealogy, race, and miscegenation to utopian contours? Why deploy the language, scenes, and tropes of paranormal fads—mesmerism, spiritualism, automatic writing, apparitions, and suspended animation—to explore the historically pressing, and often violent, expressions of racism in Jim Crow America? The answer to such a question seems much less baffling when it is read as fantasy, utopian in stripe, of a fully self-sustaining black community existing in the ancient past, meant to prefigure the reincarnation of the same such community in present-day America. Critics have been slow to grant Hopkins's novel such a reading, some agreeing with Eric Sundquist that Hopkins's "back-to-Africa" plot was a "patently escapist fiction meant to flee the brutality and racism of American history in favor of lost history of great wealth, material achievement, and intellectual superiority" (Sundquist, 569). He goes on to acknowledge, however, that her "intent was less to promote back-to-Africa philosophy than to draw from it a popularized basis for pride in black history and, more important, a theoretically complex way to understand African-American double consciousness" (Sundquist, 573).

Hopkins's African fantasy was indeed connected to a broader initiative to rewrite African history, an objective she shared with other African-American intellectuals of the day, both lay and academic. In some ways, *Of One Blood* anticipates the premises of the booklet Hopkins would later publish, *Primer of Facts Pertaining to the Early Greatness of the African Race,* her contribution to a shelf of books similarly devoted to claiming and extolling the greatness of the ancient African past. William Wells Brown's 1874 volume, *The Rising Son; or the Antecedents and Advancement of the Coloured Race,* was one such volume on which, according to Sundquist, Hopkins drew heavily in writing *Of One Blood.* The implication of Brown's work, and Hopkins's by extension, is that knowledge of their African antecedents would contribute to African-American advancement in the present day, but those antecedents had first to be excavated, specifically for the benefit of African-Americans who needed to know that they were a "branch of the wonderful and mysterious Ethiopian who had a prehistoric existence of magnificence, the full record of which is lost in obscurity." These words, spoken by Professor Stone, the British leader of the novel's African expedition, provide a clue to Hopkins's complex treatment of Telassar, which is both state of geography and state of mind, forged from Hopkins's amalgamation of black history and "the new psychology."

As a mesmerist and mystic, Reuel accepts the existence of the spirit realm. While aware, as he puts it, that "supernatural phenomena" are "best known to the everyday world as 'effects of the imagination,' a phrase of mere dismissal," he rejects that theory. Accepting that visitants from the spirit world close the boundary between life and death (and the "normal" and the "paranormal"), he also accepts that they "live" in the realm of unconscious memory and fantasy. In other words, Reuel comes ultimately to understand that Telassar, this undiscovered country of Africa, is, in essence, "the undiscovered country within ourselves—the hidden self lying quiescent in every human soul" awaiting its awakening. That this awakened African past is embodied in women—Dianthe and Candace—exposes yet another facet of Hopkins's fantasy and of her grounding metaphor of blood. It is significant that Reuel inherits his mystical powers from the maternal side of his family tree, and the lotus lily, the visual sign of that lineage, is known only by two other women in the novel: Hannah, the former slave, and the phantom Mira, her dead-yet-living daughter. That Mira manifests her presence through automatic writing in scenes in which the novel's genealogical mysteries are solved encourages us to see her as perhaps Hopkins's fantasy of female literary power, particularly at a moment when African-American men were acquiring more critical notice and acclaim in the literary realm. But such a reading is necessarily tempered by the fact that the novel mainly consigns women to merely reproductive roles. Women are primarily cast in Hopkins's novels as the bodily vessels of history, "charged with the reproduction of persons as well as the birthing of nations," according to Dana Luciano (165), including the nation of Telassar.

While clearly utopian in outline, Telassar is not, as M. Giulia Fabi has suggested, the "traditional *ou-topoi* (nonplace) of traditional utopian fiction" (47), for the threat that European colonialism poses to Telassar allegorized the historical situation of many African countries. And while Aubrey Livingston is no stand-in for the famed explorer Stanley Livingstone, it's tempting to suppose that Hopkins may have indeed intended something of a parallel between the two. Aubrey, after all, arranges the expedition that installs Reuel safely offshore, leaving Aubrey to seduce Reuel's unwitting bride, Dianthe. While Eric Sundquist is certainly not amiss in reading *Of One Blood* as "a signifying inversion of the colonial adventure story widely popular in the work of H. Rider Haggard and others" (570), the novel seems to signify more generally on the marvelous records of African exploration, on the voluminous *nonfictional* quest romances in which Promethean explorers bring light and "civilization" to the benighted "Dark Continent."

While Hopkins certainly bids to counter this myth, some aspects of her novel seem clearly to support it. After all, on the novel's last page Reuel is back in the "Hidden City" where "he spends his days in teaching his people all that he has learned in years of contact with modern culture."

While Hopkins may seem to be equivocating here, other of her contemporaries produced voluminous work devoted to proving that Africa had been "civilized" for centuries, even as the Western world was sunk in barbarism. This glorious past would reassert itself and "Ethiopia" would rise again when African-Americans restored its history to memory and consciousness and resumed their rightful and exalted places in American society. In concluding *Of One Blood* in Africa, Hopkins clearly means to evoke that strain of cultural nationalism that came to be called "Ethiopianism," even if she modifies some of its implications.

As Wilson J. Moses notes, "Ethiopianism," affiliated with the political and religious experiences of English-speaking Africans, dated back to the eighteenth and early nineteenth centuries, but it remained a vital intellectual idea among the writers of Hopkins's late-nineteenth-century generation. Derived from the Biblical passage "Princes shall come out of Egypt; Ethiopia shall soon stretch out her hands unto God" (Psalms 68:31), Ethiopianism was initially regarded, Moses notes, as a prophecy that Africa would be delivered from the "darkness of heathenism," but it came to be interpreted more widely as "a promise that Africa [would] . . . experience a dramatic political, industrial, and economic renaissance" or that the "black man [would] rule the world" (157).

Ethiopianism, like Pan-Africanism more generally, represented to Hopkins and her contemporaries a belief system of practical value, linking African-Americans to their African past and promising them a future deliverance foretold in the old Testament and inscribed in such spirituals as "Go Down Moses," which Dianthe sings throughout the book. But it could be argued that *Of One Blood* establishes, whether wittingly or not, the limits of Ethiopianism and provides a preview of what the idea became in time: mainly an empty symbol of limited practical utility and value as political bedrock. This explains in part why some readers find the resolution of Hopkins's last novel escapist. As the present and future of African-Americans —increasingly identified as a "problem"—was being hotly debated in the public sphere and the abridgement of their freedoms was de rigueur, surely a novel that trafficked in fantasy and the paranormal could seem odd. And yet it bears remembering that Hopkins was writing in the face of perhaps the most resilient fantasy in the U.S. cultural imaginary: the fantasy of "whiteness," which, it could be added, was "paranormal" in the extreme although it enjoyed a naturalized "normativity" in "scientific" discourse, as well as in the political economy of the nation.

Since Hopkins's career as a published novelist ended with *Of One Blood*, we can only speculate as to where her vivid, phantasmagoric imagination would have taken her. But her previous novels established her penchant. The vast historical expanses encompassed in Hopkins's novels consistently serve a philosophy of history that renders the past as prologue, as harbinger of emphatically urgent matters in the present. And placing Hopkins in the tradition of African-American letters, we might then see her "Hidden City" of Telassar as a version of Ralph Ellison's hero's cellar down below: as a hiatus of a kind or, in his narrator's words, "a covert preparation for more overt action."

Deborah E. McDowell

WORKS CITED

Binet, Alfred. *On Double Consciousness* in Volume 5, Series C. Medical Psychology: Significant Contributions to the History of Psychology, 1896.

DuBois, W. E. B. *The Souls of Black Folk*, ed. Henry Louis Gates Jr. and Terri Hume Oliver. New York: W. W. Norton, 1999.

Fabi, M. Giulia. *Passing and the Rise of the African American Novel*. Urbana: University of Illinois Press, 2001.

Gould, Stephen J. *The Mismeasure of Man*. New York: W. W. Norton, 1981.

Hopkins, Pauline E. *Contending Forces: A Romance Illustrative of Negro Life North and South*. 1900. New York Oxford University Press, 1988: xxvii–xlviii.

James, William. "The Hidden Self." *Scribner's Magazine* 7 (January–June 1890): 243–255.

Luciano, Dana. "Passing Shadows: Melancholic Nationality and Black Critical Publicity In Pauline E. Hopkins's *Of One Blood*" in David L. Eng and David Kazanjian, eds. *Loss: The Politics of Mourning*. Berkeley: University of California Press: 148–187.

Moses, Wilson J. *The Golden Age of Black Nationalism, 1850–1925*. New York: Oxford University Press, 1978.

Otten, Terry. "Pauline Hopkins and the Hidden Self of Race." *ELH* 59 (1922): 227–56.

Schrager, Cynthia. "The New Psychology and the Politics of Race: Pauline Hopkins and William James," in John Gruesser, ed. *The Unruly Voice: Rediscovering Pauline E. Hopkins*. Urbana: University of Illinois Press, 1996: 182–209.

Sundquist, Eric. *To Wake the Nations: Race in the Making of American Literature*. Cambridge: Harvard University Press, 1993.

Yarborough, Richard. "Introduction" to Pauline Hopkins. *Contending Forces: A Romance of Negro Life North and South*. 1900. New York: Oxford University Press, 1988: xxvii–xlviii.

OF
ONE BLOOD
Or, The Hidden Self

CHAPTER I

HE recitations were over for the day. It was the first week in November and it had rained about every day the entire week; now freezing temperature added to the discomfiture of the dismal season. The lingering equinoctial whirled the last clinging yellow leaves from the trees on the campus and strewed them over the deserted paths, while from the leaden sky fluttering snow-white flakes gave an unexpected touch of winter to the scene.

The east wind for which Boston and vicinity is celebrated, drove the sleet against the window panes of the room in which Reuel Briggs sat among his books and the apparatus for experiments. The room served for both living and sleeping. Briggs could have told you that the bareness and desolateness of the apartment were like his life, but he was a reticent man who knew how to suffer in silence. The dreary wet afternoon, the cheerless walk over West Boston bridge through the soaking streets had but served to emphasize the loneliness of his position, and morbid thoughts had haunted him all day: To what use all this persistent hard work for a place in the world—clothes, food, a roof? Is suicide wrong? he asked himself with tormenting persistency. From out the storm, voices and hands seemed beckoning him all day to cut the Gordian knot and solve the riddle of whence and whither for all time.

His place in the world would soon be filled; no vacuum remained empty; the eternal movement of all things onward closed up the gaps, and the wail of the newly-born augmented the great army of mortals pressing the vitals of mother Earth with hurrying tread. So he had tormented himself for months, but the courage was yet wanting for strength to rend the veil. It had grown dark early. Reuel had not stirred from his room since coming from the hospital—had not eaten nor drank, and was in full possession of the solitude he craved. It was now five o'clock. He sat sideways by the bare table, one leg crossed over the other. His fingers kept the book open at the page where he was reading, but his attention wandered beyond the leaden sky, the dripping panes, and the sounds of the driving storm outside.

He was thinking deeply of the words he had just read, and which the darkness had shut from his gaze. The book was called "The Unclassified Residuum," just published and eagerly sought by students of mysticism, and dealing with the great field of new discoveries in psychology. Briggs was a close student of what might be termed "absurdities" of supernatural phenomena or *mysticism*, best known to the every-day world as "effects of the imagination," a phrase of mere dismissal, and which it is impossible to make precise; the book suited the man's mood. These were the words of haunting significance:

"All the while, however, the phenomena are there, lying broadcast over the surface of history. No matter where you open its pages, you find things recorded under the name of divinations, inspirations, demoniacal possessions, apparitions, trances, ecstasies, miraculous healing and productions of disease, and occult powers possessed by peculiar individuals over persons and things in their neighborhood.

"The mind-curers and Christian scientists, who are beginning to lift up their heads in our communities, unquestionably get remarkable results in certain cases. The ordinary medical man dismisses them from his attention with the cut-and-dried remark that they are 'only the effects of the imagination.' But there is a meaning in this vaguest of phrases.

"We know a non-hysterical woman who in her trances knows facts which altogether transcend her *possible* normal consciousness, facts about the lives of people whom she never saw or heard of before. I am well aware of all the liabilities to which this statement exposes me, and I make it deliberately, having practically no doubt whatever of its truth."

Presently Briggs threw the book down, and, rising from his chair, began pacing up and down the bare room.

"That is it," at length he said aloud. "I have the power, I know the truth of every word—of all M. Binet asserts, and could I but complete the necessary experiments, I would astonish the world. O Poverty, Ostracism! have I not drained the bitter cup to the dregs!" he apostrophized, with a harsh, ironical laugh.

Mother Nature had blessed Reuel Briggs with superior physical endowments, but as yet he had never had reason to count them blessings. No one could fail to notice the vast breadth of shoulder, the strong throat that upheld a plain face, the long limbs, the sinewy hands. His head was that of an athlete, with close-set ears, and covered with an abundance of black hair, straight and closely cut, thick and smooth; the nose was the aristocratic feature, although nearly spoiled by broad nostrils, of this remarkable young man; his skin was white, but of a tint suggesting olive, an almost sallow color which is a mark of strong, melancholic temperaments. His large mouth concealed powerful long white teeth which gleamed through lips even and narrow, parting generally in a smile at once grave, genial and singularly sweet; indeed Briggs's smile changed the plain face at once into one that interested and fascinated men and women. True there were lines about the mouth which betrayed a passionate, nervous temperament, but they accorded well with the rest of his strong personality. His eyes were a very bright and piercing gray, courageous, keen and shrewd. Briggs was not a man to be despised—physically or mentally.

None of the students associated together in the hive of men under the fostering care of the "benign mother" knew aught of Reuel Briggs's origin. It was rumored at first that he was of Italian birth, then they "guessed" he was a Japanese, but whatever land claimed him as a son, all voted him a genius in his scientific studies, and much was expected of him at graduation. He had no money, for he was unsocial and shabby to the point of seediness, and apparently no relatives, for his correspondence was limited to the letters of editors of well known local papers and magazines. Somehow he lived and paid his way in a third-rate lodging-house near Harvard square, at the expense of the dull intellects or the idle rich, with which a great university always teems, to whom Briggs acted as "coach," and by contributing scientific articles to magazines on the absorbing subject of spiritualistic phenomena. A few of his articles had produced a profound impression. The monotonous pacing continued for a time, finally ending at the mantel, from whence he abstracted a disreputable looking pipe and filled it.

"Well," he soliloquized, as he reseated himself in his chair, "Fate had done her worst, but she mockingly beckons me on and I accept her challenge. I shall not yet attempt the bourne. If I conquer, it will be by strength of brain and will-power. I shall conquer; I must and will."

The storm had increased in violence; the early dusk came swiftly down, and at this point in his revery the rattling window panes, as well as the whistle and shriek of gusts of moaning wind, caught his attention. "Phew! a beastly night." With a shiver, he drew his chair closer to the cylinder stove, whose glowing body was the only cheerful object in the bare room.

As he sat with his back half-turned to catch the grateful warmth, he looked out into the dim twilight across the square and into the broad paths of the campus, watching the skeleton arms of giant trees tossing in the wind, and the dancing snow-flakes that fluttered to earth in their fairy gowns to be quickly transformed into running streams that fairly overflowed the gutters. He fell into a dreamy state as he gazed, for which he could not account. As he sent his earnest, penetrating gaze into the night, gradually the darkness and storm faded into tints of cream and rose and soft moist lips. Silhouetted against the background of lowering sky and waving branches, he saw distinctly outlined a fair face framed in golden hair, with soft brown eyes, deep and earnest—terribly earnest they seemed just then—rose-tinged baby lips, and an expression of wistful entreaty. O how real, how very real did the passing shadow appear to the gazer!

He tried to move, uneasily conscious that this strange experience was but "the effect of the imagination," but he was powerless. The unknown countenance grew dimmer and farther off, floating gradually out of sight, while a sense of sadness and foreboding wrapped him about as with a pall.

A wilder gust of wind shook the window sashes. Reuel stared about him in a bewildered way like a man awakening from a heavy sleep. He listened to the wail of the blast and glanced at the fire and rubbed his eyes. The vision was gone; he was alone in the room; all was silence and darkness. The ticking of the cheap clock on the mantel kept time with his heart-beats. The light of his own life seemed suddenly eclipsed with the passing of the lovely vision of Venus. Conscious of an odd murmur in his head, which seemed to control his movements, he rose and went toward the window to open it; there came a loud knock at the door.

Briggs did not answer at once. He wanted no company.

Perhaps the knocker would go away. But he was persistent. Again came the knock ending in a double rat-tat accompanied by the words:

"I know you are there; open, open, you son of Erebus! You inhospitable Turk!"

Thus admonished Briggs turned the key and threw wide open the door.

"It's you, is it? Confound you, you're always here when you're not wanted," he growled.

The visitor entered and closed the door behind him. With a laugh he stood his dripping umbrella back of the stove against the chimney-piece, and immediately a small stream began trickling over the uncarpeted floor; he then relieved himself of his damp outer garments.

"Son of Erebus, indeed, you ungrateful man. It's as black as Hades in this room; a light, a light! Why did you keep me waiting out there like a drowned rat?"

The voice was soft and musical. Briggs lighted the student lamp. The light revealed a tall man with the beautiful face of a Greek God; but the sculptured features did not inspire confidence. There was that in the countenance of Aubrey Livingston that engendered doubt. But he had been kind to Briggs, was, in fact, his only friend in the college, or, indeed, in the world for that matter.

By an act of generosity he had helped the forlorn youth, then in his freshman year, over obstacles which bade fair to end his college days. Although the pecuniary obligation was long since paid, the affection and worship Reuel had conceived for his deliverer was dog-like in its devotion.

"Beastly night," he continued, as he stretched his full length luxuriously in the only easy chair the room afforded. "What are you mooning about all alone in the darkness?"

"Same old thing," replied Briggs briefly.

"No wonder the men say that you have a twist, Reuel."

"Ah, man! but the problem of whence and whither! To solve it is my life; I live for that alone; let'm talk."

"You ought to be re-named the 'Science of Trance-States,' Reuel. How a man can grind day and night beats me." Livingston handed him a cigar and for a time they smoked in silence. At length Reuel said:

"Shake hands with Poverty once, Aubrey, and you will solve the secret of many a student's success in life."

"Doubtless it would do me good," replied Livingston with a laugh, "but just at present, it's the ladies, bless their sweet faces who disturb me, and not delving in books nor weeping over ways and means. Shades of my fathers, forbid that I should ever have to work!"

"Lucky dog!" growled Reuel, enviously, as he gazed admiringly at the handsome face turned up to the ceiling and gazing with soft caressing eyes at the ugly whitewashed wall through rings of curling smoke. "Yet you have a greater gift of duality than I," he added dreamily. "Say what you will; ridicule me, torment me, but you know as well as I that the wonders of a material world cannot approach those of the undiscovered country within ourselves—the hidden self lying quiescent in every human soul."

"True, Reuel, and I often wonder what becomes of the mind and morals, distinctive entities grouped in the republic known as man, when death comes. Good and evil in me contend; which will gain the mastery? Which will accompany me into the silent land?"

"Good and evil, God and the devil," suggested Reuel. "Yes, sinner or saint, body or soul, which wins in the life struggle? I am not sure that it matters which," he concluded with a shrug of his handsome shoulders. "I should know if I never saw you again until the struggle was over. Your face will tell its own tale in another five years. Now listen to this:" He caught up the book he had been reading and rapidly turning the leaves read over the various passages that had impressed him.

"A curious accumulation of data; the writer evidently takes himself seriously," Livingston commented.

"And why not?" demanded Reuel. "You and I know enough to credit the author with honest intentions."

"Yes; but are we prepared to go so far?"

"This man is himself a mystic. He gives his evidence clearly enough."

"And do you credit it?"

"Every word! Could I but get the necessary subject, I would convince you; I would go farther than M. Binet in unveiling the vast scheme of compensation and retribution carried about in the vast recesses of the human soul."

"Find the subject and I will find the money," laughed Aubrey.

"Do you mean it, Aubrey? Will you join me in carrying forward a search for more light in the mysteries of existence?"

"I mean it. And now, Reuel, come down from the clouds, and come with me to a concert."

"Tonight?"

"Yes, 'tonight,'" mimicked the other. "The blacker the night, the greater the need of amusement. You go out too little."

"Who gives the concert?"

"Well, it's a new departure in the musical world; something Northerners know nothing of; but I who am a Southerner, born and bred, or as the vulgar have it, 'dyed in the wool,' know and understand Negro music. It is a jubilee concert given by a party of Southern colored people at Tremont Temple. I have the tickets. Redpath has them in charge."

"Well, if you say so, I suppose I must." Briggs did not seem greatly impressed.

"Coming down to the practical, Reuel, what do you think of the Negro problem? Come to think of it, I have never heard you express an opinion about it. I believe it is the only burning question in the whole category of live issues and ologies about which you are silent."

"I have a horror of discussing the woes of unfortunates, tramps, stray dogs and cats and Negroes—probably because I am an unfortunate myself."

They smoked in silence.

CHAPTER II

HE passing of slavery from the land marked a new era in the life of the nation. The war, too, had passed like a dream of horrors, and over the resumption of normal conditions in business and living, the whole country, as one man, rejoiced and heaved a deep sigh of absolute content.

Under the spur of the excitement occasioned by the Proclamation of Freedom, and the great need of schools for the blacks, thousands of dollars were contributed at the North, and agents were sent to Great Britain, where generosity towards the Negroes was boundless. Money came from all directions, pouring into the hands of philanthropists, who were anxious to prove that the country was able, not only to free the slave, but to pay the great debt it owed him,— protection as he embraced freedom, and a share in the great Government he had aided to found by sweat and toil and blood. It was soon discovered that the Negro possessed a phenomenal gift of music, and it was determined to utilize this gift in helping to support educational institutions of color in the Southland.

A band of students from Fisk University were touring the country, and those who had been fortunate enough to listen once to their matchless untrained voices singing their heartbreaking minor music with its grand and impossible intervals and sound combinations, were eager to listen again and yet again.

Wealthy and exclusive society women everywhere vied in

11

showering benefits and patronage upon the new prodigies who had suddenly become the pets of the musical world. The Temple was a blaze of light, and crowded from pit to dome. It was the first appearance of the troupe in New England, therefore it was a gala night, and Boston culture was out in force.

The two friends easily found their seats in the first balcony, and from that position idly scanned the vast audience to beguile the tedious waiting. Reuel's thoughts were disturbed; he read over the program, but it carried no meaning to his pre-occupied mind; he was uneasy; the face he had seen outlined in the twilight haunted him. A great nervous dread of he knew not what possessed him, and he actually suffered as he sat there answering at random the running fire of comments made by Livingston on the audience, and replying none too cordially to the greetings of fellow-students, drawn to the affair, like himself, by curiosity.

"Great crowd for such a night," observed one. "The weather matches your face, Briggs; why didn't you leave it outside? Why do you look so down?"

Reuel shrugged his shoulders.

"They say there are some pretty girls in the troup; one or two as white as we," continued the speaker unabashed by Reuel's surliness.

"They range at home from alabaster to ebony," replied Livingston. "The results of amalgamation are worthy the careful attention of all medical experts."

"Don't talk shop, Livingston," said Briggs peevishly.

"You are really more disagreeable than usual," replied Livingston, pleasantly. "Do try to be like the other fellows, for once, Reuel."

Silence ensued for a time, and then the irrepressible one of the party remarked: "The soprano soloist is great; heard her in New York." At this there was a general laugh among the men.

Good natured Charlie Vance was generally "struck" once a month with the "loveliest girl, by jove, you know."

"That explains your presence here, Vance; what's her name?"

"Dianthe Lusk."

"Great name. I hope she comes up to it,—the flower of Jove."

"Flower of Jove, indeed! You'll say so when you see her," cried Charlie with his usual enthusiasm.

"What! again, my son? 'Like Dian's kiss, unmasked, unsought, Love gives itself' " quoted Livingston, with a smile on his handsome face.

"Oh, stow it! Aubrey, even your cold blood will be stirred at sight of her exquisite face; of her voice I will not speak; I cannot do it justice."

"If this is to be the result of emancipation, I for one vote that we ask Congress to annul the Proclamation," said Reuel, drily.

Now conversation ceased; a famous local organist began a concert on the organ to occupy the moments of waiting. The music soothed Reuel's restlessness. He noticed that the platform usually occupied by the speaker's desk, now held a number of chairs and a piano. Certainly, the assiduous advertising had brought large patronage for the new venture, he thought as he idly calculated the financial result from the number in the audience.

Soon the hot air, the glare of lights, the mingling of choice perfumes emanating from the dainty forms of elegantly attired women, acted upon him as an intoxicant. He began to feel the pervading excitement—the flutter of expectation, and presently the haunting face left him.

The prelude drew to a close; the last chord fell from the fingers of the artist; a line of figures—men and women—dark in hue, and neatly dressed in quiet evening clothes, filed noiselessly from the ante-rooms and filled the chairs upon the platform. The silence in the house was painful. These were representatives of the people for whom God had sent the terrible scourge of blood upon the land to free from bondage. The old abolitionists in the vast audience felt the blood leave their faces beneath the stress of emotion.

The opening number was "The Lord's Prayer." Stealing, rising, swelling, gathering, as it thrilled the ear, all the delights of harmony in a grand minor cadence that told of deliverance from bondage and homage to God for his wonderful aid, sweeping the awed heart with an ecstasy that was almost pain; breathing, hovering, soaring, they held the vast multitude in speechless wonder.

Thunders of applause greeted the close of the hymn. Scarcely waiting for a silence, a female figure rose and came slowly to the edge of the platform and stood in the blaze of lights with hands modestly clasped before her. She was not in any way the preconceived idea of a Negro. Fair as the fairest woman in the hall, with wavy bands of chestnut hair, and great, melting eyes of brown, soft as those of childhood; a willowy figure of exquisite mould, clad in a sombre gown of black. There fell a voice upon the listening ear, in celestial showers of silver that passed all conceptions, all comparisons, all dreams; a voice beyond belief—a great soprano of unimaginable beauty, soaring heavenward in mighty intervals.

"Go down, Moses, way down in Egypt's land, Tell ol' Pharaoh, let my people go," sang the woman in tones that awakened ringing harmonies in the heart of every listener.

"By Jove!" Reuel heard Livingston exclaim. For himself he was dazed, thrilled; never save among the great artists of the earth, was such a voice heard alive with the divine fire.

Some of the women in the audience wept; there was the distinct echo of a sob in the deathly quiet which gave tribute to the power of genius. Spell-bound they sat beneath the outpoured anguish of a suffering soul. All the horror, the degradation from which a race had been delivered were in the pleading strains of the singer's voice. It strained the senses almost beyond endurance. It pictured to that self-possessed, highly-cultured New England assemblage as nothing else ever had, the awfulness of the hell from which a people had been happily plucked.

Reuel was carried out of himself; he leaned forward in eager contemplation of the artist; he grew cold with terror and fear. Surely it could not be—he must be dreaming! It was incredible! Even as he whispered the words to himself the hall seemed to grow dim and shadowy; the sea of faces melted away; there before him in the blaze of light—like a lovely phantom—stood a woman wearing the face of his vision of the afternoon!

CHAPTER III

T was Hallow-eve.

The north wind blew a cutting blast over the stately Charles, and broke the waves into a miniature flood; it swept the streets of the University city, and danced on into the outlying suburbs tossing the last leaves about in gay disorder, not even sparing the quiet precincts of Mount Auburn cemetery. A deep, clear, moonless sky stretched overhead, from which hung myriads of sparkling stars.

In Mount Auburn, where the residences of the rich lay far apart, darkness and quietness had early settled down. The main street seemed given over to the duskiness of the evening, and with one exception, there seemed no light on earth or in heaven save the cold gleam of the stars.

The one exception was in the home of Charlie Vance, or "Adonis," as he was called by his familiars. The Vance estate was a spacious house with rambling ells, tortuous chimney-stacks, and corners, eaves and ledges; the grounds were extensive and well kept telling silently of the opulence of its owner. Its windows sent forth a cheering light. Dinner was just over.

Within, on an old-fashioned hearth, blazed a glorious wood fire, which gave a rich coloring to the oak-panelled walls, and fell warmly on a group of young people seated and standing, chatting about the fire. At one side of it, in a chair of the Elizabethan period, sat the hostess, Molly Vance, only daughter

17

of James Vance, Esq., and sister of "Adonis," a beautiful girl of eighteen.

At the opposite side, leaning with folded arms against the high carved mantel, stood Aubrey Livingston; the beauty of his fair hair and blue eyes was never more marked as he stood there in the gleam of the fire and the soft candle light. He was talking vivaciously, his eyes turning from speaker to speaker, as he ran on, but resting chiefly with pride on his beautiful betrothed, Molly Vance.

The group was completed by two or three other men, among them Reuel Briggs, and three pretty girls. Suddenly a clock struck the hour.

"Only nine," exclaimed Molly. "good people, what shall we do to wile the tedium of waiting for the witching hour? Have any one of you enough wisdom to make a suggestion?"

"Music," said Livingston.

"We don't want anything so commonplace."

"Blind Man's Buff," suggested "Adonis."

"Oh! please not that, the men are so rough!"

"Let us," broke in Cora Scott, "tell ghost stories."

"Good, Cora! yes, yes, yes."

"No, no!" exclaimed a chorus of voices.

"Yes, yes," laughed Molly, gaily, clapping her hands. "It is the very thing. Cora, you are the wise woman of the party. It is the very time, tonight is the new moon, and we can try our projects in the Hyde house."

"The moon should be full to account for such madness," said Livingston.

"Don't be disagreeable, Aubrey," replied Molly. "The 'ayes' have it. You're with me, Mr. Briggs?"

"Of course, Miss Vance," answered Reuel, "to go to the

North Pole or Hades—only please tell us where is Hyde house.' "

"Have you never heard? Why it's the adjoining estate. It is reputed to be haunted, and a lady in white haunts the avenue in the most approved ghostly style."

"Bosh!" said Livingston.

"Possibly," remarked the laughing Molly, "but it is the 'bosh' of a century."

"Go on, Miss Vance; don't mind Aubrey. Who has seen the lady?"

"She is not easily seen," proceeded Molly, "she only appears on Hallow-eve, when the moon is new, as it will be tonight. I had forgotten that fact when I invited you here. If anyone stands, tonight, in the avenue leading to the house, he will surely see the tall veiled figure gliding among the old hemlock trees."

One or two shivered.

"If, however, the watcher remain, the lady will pause, and utter some sentence of prophecy of his future."

"Has any one done this?" queried Reuel.

"My old nurse says she remembers that the lady was seen once."

"Then, we'll test it again tonight!" exclaimed Reuel, greatly excited over the chance to prove his pet theories.

"Well, Molly, you've started Reuel off on his greatest hobby; I wash my hands of both of you."

"Let us go any way!" chorused the venturesome party.

"But there are conditions," exclaimed Molly. "Only one person must go at a time."

Aubrey laughed as he noticed the consternation in one or two faces.

"So," continued Molly, "as we cannot go together, I propose

that each shall stay a quarter of an hour, then whether successful or not, return and let another take his or her place. I will go
first."

"No—" it was Charlie who spoke—"I put my veto on that,
Molly, If you are mad enough to risk colds in this mad freak, it
shall be done fairly. We will draw lots."

"And I add to that, not a girl leave the house; we men will
try the charm for the sake of your curiosity, but not a girl goes.
You can try the ordinary Hallow-eve projects while we are
away."

With many protests, but concealed relief, this plan was
reluctantly adopted by the female element. The lots were prepared and placed in a hat, and amid much merriment, drawn.

"You are third, Mr. Briggs," exclaimed Molly who held the
hat and watched the checks.

"I'm first," said Livingston, "and Charlie second."

"While we wait for twelve, tell us the story of the house,
Molly," cried Cora.

Thus adjured, Molly settled herself comfortably in her chair
and began: "Hyde House is nearly opposite the cemetery, and its
land joins that of this house; it is indebted for its ill-repute to
one of its owners, John Hyde. It has been known for years as a
haunted house, and avoided as such by the superstitious. It is
low-roofed, rambling, and almost entirely concealed by hemlocks, having an air of desolation and decay in keeping with its
ill-repute. In its dozen rooms were enacted the dark deeds which
gave the place the name of the 'haunted house.'

"The story is told of an unfaithful husband, a wronged wife
and a beautiful governess forming a combination which led to
the murder of a guest for his money. The master of the house
died from remorse, under peculiar circumstances. These materi-
als give us the plot for a thrilling ghost story."

"Well, where does the lady come in?" interrupted "Adonis."

There was a general laugh.

"This world is all a blank without the ladies for Charlie," remarked Aubrey. "Molly, go on with your story, my child."

"You may all laugh as much as you please, but what I am telling you is believed in this section by every one. A local magazine speaks of it as follows, as near as I can remember:

" 'A most interesting story is told by a woman who occupied the house for a short time. She relates that she had no sooner crossed the threshold than she was met by a beautiful woman in flowing robes of black, who begged permission to speak through her to her friends. The friends were thereupon bidden to be present at a certain time. When all were assembled they were directed by invisible powers to kneel. Then the spirit told the tale of the tragedy through the woman. The spirit was the niece of the murderer, and she was in the house when the crime was committed. She discovered blood stains on the door of the woodshed, and told her uncle that she suspected him of murdering the guest, who had mysteriously disappeared. He secured her promise not to betray him. She had always kept the secret. Although both had been dead for many years, they were chained to the scene of the crime, as was the governess, who was the man's partner in guilt. The final release of the niece from the place was conditional on her making a public confession. This done she would never be heard from again. And she never was, except on Hallow-eve, when the moon is new.' "

"Bring your science and philosophy to bear on this, Reuel. Come, come, man, give us your opinion," exclaimed Aubrey.

"Reuel doesn't believe such stuff; he's too sensible," added Charlie.

"If these are facts, they are only for those who have a mental affinity with them. I believe that if we could but strengthen our mental sight, we could discover the broad highway between this and the other world on which both good and evil travel to earth," replied Reuel.

"And that first highway was beaten out of chaos by Satan, as Milton has it, eh, Briggs?"

"Have it as you like, Smith. No matter. For my own part, I have never believed that the whole mental world is governed by the faculties we understand, and can reduce to reason or definite feelings. But I will keep my ideas to myself; one does not care to be laughed at."

The conversation was kept up for another hour about indifferent subjects, but all felt the excitement underlying the frivolous chatter. At quarter before twelve, Aubrey put on his ulster with the words: "Well, here goes for my lady." The great doors were thrown open, and the company grouped about him to see him depart.

"Mind, honor bright, you go," laughed Charlie.

"Honor bright," he called back.

Then he went on beyond the flood of light into the gloom of the night. Muffled in wraps and ulsters they lingered on the piazzas waiting his return.

"Would he see anything?"

"Of course not!" laughed Charlie and Bert Smith. "Still, we bet he'll be sharp to his time."

They were right. Aubrey returned at five minutes past twelve, a failure.

Charlie ran down the steps briskly, but in ten minutes came hastening back.

"Well," was the chorus, "did you see it?"

"I saw something—a figure in the trees!"

"And you did not wait?" said Molly, scornfully.

"No, I dared not; I own it."

"It's my turn; I'm third," said Reuel.

"Luck to you, old man," they called as he disappeared in the darkness.

Reuel Briggs was a brave man. He knew his own great physical strength and felt no fear as he traversed the patch of woods lying between the two estates. As he reached the avenue of hemlocks he was not thinking of his mission, but of the bright home scene he had just left—of love and home and rest—such a life as was unfolding before Aubrey Livingston and sweet Molly Vance.

"I suppose there are plenty of men in the world as lonely as I am," he mused; "but I suppose it is my own fault. A man though plain and poor can generally manage to marry; and I am both. But I don't regard a wife as one regards bread—better sour bread than starvation; better an uncongenial life-companion than none! What a frightful mistake! No! The woman I marry must be to me a necessity, because I love her; because so loving her, 'all the current of my being flows to her,' and I feel she is my supreme need."

Just now he felt strangely happy as he moved in the gloom of the hemlocks, and he wondered many times after that whether the spirit is sometimes mysteriously conscious of the nearness of its kindred spirit; and feels, in anticipation, the "sweet unrest" of the master-passion that rules the world.

The mental restlessness of three weeks before seemed to have possession of him again. Suddenly the "restless, unsatisfied longing," rose again in his heart. He turned his head and saw a female figure just ahead of him in the path, coming toward him. He could not see her features distinctly, only the eyes—large, bright and dark. But their expression! Sorrowful, wistful—almost imploring—gazing straightforward, as if they saw nothing—like the eyes of a person entirely absorbed and not distinguishing one object from another.

She was close to him now, and there was a perceptible pause in her step. Suddenly she covered her face with her clasped hands, as if in uncontrollable grief. Moved by a mighty emotion, Briggs addressed the lonely figure:

"You are in trouble, madam; may I help you?"

Briggs never knew how he survived the next shock. Slowly the hands were removed from the face and the moon gave a distinct view of the lovely features of the jubilee singer—Dianthe Lusk.

She did not seem to look at Briggs, but straight before her, as she said in a low, clear, passionless voice:

"You can help me, but not now; tomorrow."

Reuel's most prominent feeling was one of delight. The way was open to become fully acquainted with the woman who had haunted him sleeping and waking for weeks past.

"Not now! Yet you are suffering. Shall I see you soon? Forgive me—but oh! tell me—"

He was interrupted. The lady moved or floated away from him, with her face toward him and gazing steadily at him.

He felt that his whole heart was in his eyes, yet hers did not drop, or did her cheek color.

"The time is not yet," she said in the same, clear, calm, measured tones, in which she had spoken before. Reuel made a quick movement toward her, but she raised her hand, and the gesture forbade him to follow her. He paused involuntarily, and she turned away, and disappeared among the gloomy hemlock trees.

He parried the questions of the merry crowd when he returned to the house, with indifferent replies. How they would have laughed at him—slave of a passion as sudden and romantic as that of Romeo for Juliet; with no more foundation than the "presentments" in books which treat of the "occult." He dropped asleep at last, in the early morning hours, and lived over his experience in his dreams.

CHAPTER IV

ALTHOUGH not yet a practitioner, Reuel Briggs was a recognized power in the medical profession. In brain diseases he was an authority.

Early the next morning he was aroused from sleep by imperative knocking at his door. It was a messenger from the hospital. There had been a train accident on the Old Colony road, would he come immediately?

Scarcely giving himself time for a cup of coffee, he arrived at the hospital almost as soon as the messenger.

The usual silence of the hospital was broken; all was bustle and movement, without confusion. It was a great call upon the resources of the officials, but they were equal to it. The doctors passed from sufferer to sufferer, dressing their injuries; then they were borne to beds from which some would never rise again.

"Come with me to the women's ward, Doctor Briggs," said a nurse. "There is a woman there who was taken from the wreck. She shows no sign of injury, but the doctors cannot restore her to consciousness. Doctor Livingston pronounces her dead, but it doesn't seem possible. So young, so beautifully. Do something for her, Doctor."

The men about a cot made way for Reuel, as he entered the ward. "It's no use Briggs," said Livingston to him in reply to his question. "Your science won't save her. The poor girl is already cold and stiff."

He moved aside disclosing to Reuel's gaze the lovely face of Dianthe Lusk!

The most marvelous thing to watch is the death of a person. At that moment the opposite takes place to that which took place when life entered the first unit, after nature had prepared it for the inception of life. How the vigorous life watches the passage of the liberated life out of its earthly environment! What a change is this! How important the knowledge of whither life tends! Here is shown the setting free of a disciplined spirit giving up its mortality for immortality,—the condition necessary to know God. Death! There is no death. Life is everlasting, and from its reality can have no end. Life is real and never changes, but preserves its identity eternally as the angels, and the immortal spirit of man, which are the only realities and continuities in the universe, God being over all, Supreme Ruler and Divine Essence from whom comes all life. Somewhat in this train ran Reuel's thoughts as he stood beside the seeming dead girl, the cynosure of all the medical faculty there assembled.

To the majority of those men, the case was an ordinary death, and that was all there was to it. What did this young upstart expect to make of it? Of his skill and wonderful theories they had heard strange tales, but they viewed him coldly as we are apt to view those who dare to leave the beaten track of conventiqnality.

Outwardly cool and stolid, showing no sign of recognition, he stood for some seconds gazing down on Dianthe; every nerve quivered, every pulse of his body throbbed. Her face held for him a wonderful charm, an extraordinary fascination. As he gazed he knew that once more he beheld what he had vaguely sought and yearned for all his forlorn life. His whole heart went out to her; destiny, not chance, had brought him to her. He saw, too, that no one knew her, none had a clue to her identity; he determined to remain silent for the present, and immediately he sought to impress Livingston to do likewise.

His keen glance swept the faces of the surrounding physicians. "No, not one," he told himself, "holds the key to unlock this seeming sleep of death." He alone could do it. Advancing far afield in the mysterious regions of science, he had stumbled upon the solution of one of life's problems: *the reanimation of the body after seeming death.*

He had hesitated to tell of his discovery to any one; not even to Livingston had he hinted of the daring possibility, fearing ridicule in case of a miscarriage in his calculations. But for the sake of this girl he would make what he felt to be a premature disclosure of the results of his experiments. Meantime, Livingston, from his place at the foot of the cot, watched his friend with fascinated eyes. He, too, had resolved, contrary to his first intention, not to speak of his knowledge of the beautiful patient's identity. Curiosity was on tiptoe; expectancy was in the air. All felt that something unusual was about to happen.

Now Reuel, with gentle fingers, touched rapidly the clammy brow, the icy, livid hands, the region of the pulseless heart. No breath came from between the parted lips; the life-giving organ was motionless. As he concluded his examination, he turned to the assembled doctors:

"As I diagnose this case, it is one of suspended animation. This woman has been long and persistently subjected to mesmeric influences, and the nervous shock induced by the excitement of the accident has thrown her into a cataleptic sleep."

"But, man!" broke from the head physician in tones of exasperation, "rigor mortis in unmistakable form is here. The woman is dead!"

At these words there was a perceptible smile on the faces of some of the students—associates who resented his genius as a personal affront, and who considered these words as good as a reprimand for the daring student, and a settler of his pretensions. Malice and envy, from Adam's time until today, have loved a shining mark.

But the reproof was unheeded. Reuel was not listening. Absorbed in thoughts of the combat before him, he was oblivious to all else as he bent over the lifeless figure on the cot. He was full of an earnest purpose. He was strung up to a high tension of force and energy. As he looked down upon the unconscious girl whom none but he could save from the awful fate of a death by post-mortem, and who by some mysterious mesmeric affinity existing between them, had drawn him to her rescue, he felt no fear that he should fail.

Suddenly he bent down and took both cold hands into his left and passed his right hand firmly over her arms from shoulder to wrist. He repeated the movements several times; there was no response to the passes. He straightened up, and again stood silently gazing upon the patient. Then, like a man just aroused from sleep, he looked across the bed at Livingston and said abruptly:

"Dr. Livingston, will you go over to my room and bring me the case of vials in my medicine cabinet? I cannot leave the patient at this point."

Livingston started in surprise as he replied: "Certainly, Briggs, if it will help you any."

"The patient does not respond to any of the ordinary methods of awakening. She would probably lie in this sleep for months, and death ensue from exhaustion, if stronger remedies are not used to restore the vital force to a normal condition."

Livingston left the hospital; he could not return under an hour; Reuel took up his station by the bed whereon was stretched an apparently lifeless body, and the other doctors went the rounds of the wards attending to their regular routine of duty. The nurses gazed at him curiously; the head doctor, upon whom the young student's earnestness and sincerity had evidently made an impression, came a number of times to the bare little room to gaze upon its silent occupants, but there was nothing new. When Livingston returned, the group again gathered about the iron cot where lay the patient.

"Gentlemen," said Reuel, with quiet dignity, when they were once more assembled, "will you individually examine the patient once more and give your verdicts?"

Once more doctors and students carefully examined the inanimate figure in which the characteristics of death were still more pronounced. On the outskirts of the group hovered the house-surgeon's assistants ready to transport the body to the operating room for the post-mortem. Again the head physician spoke, this time impatiently.

"We are wasting our time, Dr. Briggs; I pronounce the woman dead. She was past medical aid when brought here."

"There is no physical damage, apparent or hidden, that you can see, Doctor?" questioned Reuel, respectfully.

"No; it is a perfectly healthful organism, though delicate. I agree entirely with your assertion that death was induced by the shock."

"Not *death*, Doctor," protested Briggs.

"Well, well, call it what you like—call it what you like, it amounts to the same in the end," replied the doctor testily.

"Do you all concur in Doctor Hamilton's diagnosis?" Briggs included all the physicians in his sweeping glance. There was a general assent.

"I am prepared to show you that in some cases of seeming death—or even death in reality— consciousness may be restored or the dead brought back to life. I have numberless times in the past six months restored consciousness to dogs and cats after rigor mortis had set in," he declared calmly.

"Bosh!" broke from a leading surgeon. In this manner the astounding statement, made in all seriousness, was received by the group of scientists mingled with an astonishment that resembled stupidity. But in spite of their scoffs, the young student's confident manner made a decided impression upon his listeners, unwilling as they were to be convinced.

Reuel went on rapidly; his eyes kindled; his whole person took on the majesty of conscious power, and pride in the knowledge he possessed. "I have found by research that life is not dependent upon organic function as a principle. It may be infused into organized bodies even after the organs have ceased to perform their legitimate offices. Where death has been due to causes which have not impaired or injured or destroyed tissue formation or torn down the structure of vital organs, life may be recalled when it has become entirely extinct, which is not so in the present case. This I have discovered by my experiments in animal magnetism."

The medical staff was fairly bewildered. Again Dr. Hamilton spoke:

"You make the assertion that the dead can be brought to life, if I understand your drift, Dr. Briggs, and you expect us to believe such utter nonsense." He added significantly, "My colleagues and I are here to be convinced."

"If you will be patient for a short time longer, Doctor, I will support my assertion by action. The secret of life lies in what we call volatile magnetism—it exists in the free atmosphere. You, Dr. Livingston, understand my meaning; do you see the possibility in my words?" he questioned, appealing to Aubrey for the first time.

"I have a faint conception of your meaning, certainly," replied his friend.

"This subtile magnetic agent is constantly drawn into the body through the lungs, absorbed and held in bounds until chemical combination has occurred through the medium of mineral agents always present in normal animal tissue. When respiration ceases this magnetism cannot be drawn into the lungs. It must be artificially supplied. This, gentlemen, is my discovery. I supply this magnetism. I have it here in the case Dr. Livingston has kindly brought me." He held up to their gaze a small phial wherein reposed a powder. Physicians and students, now eager listeners, gazed spell-bound upon him, straining their ears to catch every tone of the low voice and every change of the luminous eyes; they pressed forward to examine the contents of the bottle. It passed from eager hand to eager hand, then back to the owner.

"This compound, gentlemen, is an exact reproduction of the conditions existing in the human body. It has common salt for its basis. This salt is saturated with oleo resin and then exposed for several hours in an atmosphere of free ammonia. The product becomes a powder, and *that* brings back the seeming dead to life."

"Establish your theory by practical demonstration, Dr. Briggs, and the dreams of many eminent practitioners will be realized," said Dr. Hamilton, greatly agitated by his words.

"Your theory smacks of the supernatural, Dr. Briggs, charlatanism, or dreams of lunacy," said the surgeon. "We leave such assertions to quacks, generally, for the time of miracles is past."

"The supernatural presides over man's formation always," returned Reuel, quietly. "Life is that evidence of supernatural endowment which originally entered nature during the formation of the units for the evolution of man. Perhaps the superstitious masses came nearer to solving the mysteries of creation than the favored elect will ever come. Be that as it may, I will not contend. I will proceed with the demonstration."

There radiated from the speaker the potent presence of a truthful mind, a pure, unselfish nature, and that inborn dignity which repels the shafts of lower minds as ocean's waves absorb the drops of rain. Something like respect mingled with awe hushed the sneers, changing them into admiration as he calmly proceeded to administer the so-called life-giving powder. Each man's watch was in his hand; one minute passed—another—and still another. The body remained inanimate.

A cold smile of triumph began to dawn on the faces of the older members of the profession, but it vanished in its incipiency, for a tremor plainly passed over the rigid form before them. Another second—another convulsive movement of the chest!

"She moves!" cried Aubrey at last carried out of himself by the strain on his nerves. "Look, gentlemen, she breathes! *She is alive;* Briggs is right! Wonderful! Wonderful!"

"We said there could not be another miracle, and here it is!" exclaimed Dr. Hamilton with strong emotion.

Five minutes more and the startled doctors fell back from the bedside at a motion of Reuel's hand. A wondering nurse, with dilated eyes, unfolded a screen, placed it in position and came and stood beside the bed opposite Reuel. Holding Dianthe's hands, he said in a low voice: "Are you awake?" Her eyes unclosed in a cold, indifferent stare which gradually changed to one of recognition. She looked at him—she smiled, and said in a weak voice, "Oh, it is you; I dreamed of you while I slept."

She was like a child—so trusting that it went straight to the young man's heart and for an instant a great lump seemed to rise in his throat and choke him. He held her hands and chafed them, but spoke with his eyes only. The nurse said in a low voice: "Dr. Briggs, a few spoonfuls of broth will help her?"

"Yes, thank you, nurse; that will be just right." He drew a chair close beside the bed, bathed her face with water and pushed back the tangle of bright hair. He felt a great relief and quiet joy that his experiment had been successful.

"Have I been ill? Where am I?" she asked after a pause, as her face grew troubled and puzzled.

"No, but you have been asleep for a long time; we grew anxious about you. You must not talk until you are stronger."

The muse returned with the broth; Dianthe drank it eagerly and called for water, then with her hand still clasped in Reuel's she sank into a deep sleep, breathing softly like a tired child. It was plain to the man of science that hope for the complete restoration of her faculties would depend upon time, nature and constitution. Her effort to collect her thoughts was unmistakable. In her sleep, presently, from her lips fell incoherent words and phrases; but through it all she clung to Reuel's hand, seeming to recognize in him a friend.

A little later the doctors filed in noiselessly and stood about the bed gazing down upon the sleeper with awe, listening to her breathing, feeling lightly the fluttering pulse. Then they left the quiet house of suffering, marvelling at the miracle just accomplished in their presence. Livingston lingered with Briggs after the other physicians were gone.

"This is a great day for you, Reuel," he said, as he laid a light caressing hand upon the other's shoulder.

Reuel seized the hand in a quick convulsive clasp. "True and tried friend, do not credit me more than I deserve. No praise is due me. I am an instrument—how I know not—a child of circumstances. Do you not perceive something strange in this case? Can you not deduce conclusions from your own intimate knowledge of this science?"

"What can you mean, Reuel?"

"I mean—it is a *dual* mesmeric trance! The girl is only partly normal now. Binet speaks at length of this possibility in his treatise. We have stumbled upon an extraordinary case. It will take a year to restore her to perfect health."

"In the meantime we ought to search out her friends."

"Is there any hurry, Aubrey?" pleaded Reuel, anxiously.

"Why not wait until her memory returns; it will not be long, I believe, although she may still be liable to the trances."

"We'll put off the evil day to any date you may name, Briggs; for my part, I would preserve her incognito indefinitely."

Reuel made no reply. Livingston was not sure that he heard him.

CHAPTER V

 HE world scarcely estimates the service rendered by those who have unlocked the gates of sensation by the revelations of science; and yet it is to the clear perception of things which we obtain by the study of nature's laws that we are enabled to appreciate her varied gifts. The scientific journals of the next month contained wonderful and *wondering* (?) accounts of the now celebrated case,—re-animation after seeming death. Reuel's lucky star was in the ascendant; fame and fortune awaited him; he had but to grasp them. Classmates who had once ignored him now sought familiar association, or else gazed upon him with awe and reverence. "How did he do it? was the query in each man's mind, and then came a stampede for all scientific matter bearing upon animal magnetism.

How often do we look in wonder at the course of other men's lives, whose paths have diverged so widely from the beaten track of our own, that, unable to comprehend the one spring upon which, perhaps, the whole secret of the diversity hinged, we have been fain to content ourselves with summing up our judgment in the common phrase, "Well, it's very strange; what odd people there are in the world to be sure!"

Many times this trite sentence was uttered during the next few months, generally terminating every debate among medical students in various colleges.

Unmindful of his growing popularity, Reuel devoted every

moment of his spare time to close study of his patient. Although but a youth, the scientist might have passed for any age under fifty, and life for him seemed to have taken on a purely mechanical aspect since he had become first in this great cause. Under pretended indifference to public criticism, throbbed a heart of gold, sensitive to a fault; desiring above all else the well-being of all humanity; his faithfulness to those who suffered amounted to complete self-sacrifice. Absolutely free from the vices which beset most young men of his age and profession, his daily life was a white, unsullied page to the friend admitted to unrestricted intercourse, and gave an irresistible impetus to that friendship, for Livingston could not but admire the newly developed depths of a nobility which he now saw unfolding day by day in Reuel's character. Nor was Livingston far behind the latter in his interest in all that affected Dianthe. Enthused by its scientific aspect, he vied with Reuel in close attention to the medical side of the case, and being more worldly did not neglect the material side.

He secretly sought out and obtained the address of the manager of the jubilee singers and to his surprise received the information that Miss Lusk had left the troupe to enter the service of a traveling magnetic physician—a woman—for a large salary. They (the troupe) were now in Europe and heard nothing of Miss Lusk since.

After receiving this information by cable, Livingston sat a long time smoking and thinking: people often disappeared in a great city, and the police would undoubtedly find the magnetic physician if he applied to them. Of course that was the sensible thing to do, but then the publicity, and he hated that for the girl's sake. Finally he decided to compromise the matter by employing a detective. With him to decide that it was expedient to do a certain thing was the same as to act; before night the case was in the hands of an expert detective who received a goodly retainer. Two weeks from that day—it was December twenty-fourth—before he left his boarding place, the detective was announced. He had found the woman in a small town near Chicago. She said that she had no knowledge of Miss Lusk's whereabouts. Dianthe had remained with her three weeks, and at the end of that time had mysteriously disappeared; she had not heard of her since.

Livingston secured the woman's name and address, gave the man a second check together with an admonition to keep silence concerning Miss Lusk. That closed the episode. But of his observations and discoveries, Aubrey said nothing, noting every phase of this strange happening in silence.

Strangely enough, none of the men that had admired the colored artist who had enthralled their senses by her wonderful singing a few weeks before, recognized her in the hospital waif consecrated to the service of science. Her incognito was complete.

The patient was now allowed the freedom of the corridors for exercise, and was about her room during the day. The returns of the trance-state were growing less regular, although she frequently fell into convulsions, thereby enduring much suffering, sometimes lying for hours in a torpid state. Livingston had never happened to be present on these occasions, but he had heard of them from eye-witnesses. One day he entered the room while one was occurring. His entrance was unnoticed as he approached lightly over the uncarpeted floor, and stood transfixed by the scene before him.

Dianthe stood upright, with closed eyes, in the middle of the room. Only the movement of her bosom betrayed breath. The other occupants of the room preserved a solemn silence. She addressed Reuel, whose outstretched arms were extended as if in blessing over her head.

"Oh! Dearest friend! hasten to cure me of my sufferings. Did you not promise at that last meeting? You said to me, 'You are in trouble and I can help you.' And I answered, 'The time is not yet.' Is it not so?"

"Yes," replied Reuel. "Patience a while longer; all will be well with you."

"Give me the benefit of your powerful will," she continued. "I know much but as yet have not the power to express it: I see much clearly, much dimly, of the powers and influences behind the Veil, and yet I cannot name them. Some time the full power will be mine; and mine shall be thine. In seven months the sick will be restored—she will awake to worldly cares once more." Her voice ceased; she sank upon the cot in a recumbent position. Her face was pale; she appeared to sleep. Fifteen minutes passed in death-like stillness, then she extended her arms, stretched, yawned, rubbed her eyes—awoke.

Livingston listened and looked in a trance of delight, his keen artistic sense fully aroused and appreciative, feeling the glamour of her presence and ethereal beauty like a man poring over a poem that he has unexpectedly stumbled upon, losing himself in it, until it becomes, as it were, a part of himself. He felt as he watched her that he was doing a foolish thing in thus exposing himself to temptation while his honor and faith were pledged to another. But then, foolishness is so much better than wisdom, particularly to a man in certain stages of life. And then he fell to questioning if there could be temptation for him through this girl—he laughed at the thought and the next instant dismay covered him with confusion, for like a flash he realized that the mischief was already done.

As we have already hinted, Aubrey was no saint; he knew that fickleness was in his blood; he had never denied himself anything that he wanted very much in his whole life. Would he grow to want this beautiful woman very much? Time would tell.

*   *   *   *   *

It was Christmas-time—a good, sensible seasonable day before Christmas, with frost and ice in abundance, and a clear, bright, wintry sky above. Boston was very full of people—mostly suburban visitors—who were rushing here and there bent on emptying their purses on the least provocation. Good-nature prevailed among the pedestrians; one poor wretch stood shivering, with blue, wan face, on the edge of the sidewalk, his sightless eyes staring straight before him, trying to draw a tune from a consumptive violin—the embodiment of despair. He was, after all, in the minority, to judge by the hundreds of comfortably-clad forms that hurried past him, breathing an atmosphere of peace and prosperity.

Tomorrow the church bells would ring out tidings that another Christmas was born, bidding all rejoice.

This evening, at six o'clock, the two friends went to dine in a hotel in a fashionable quarter. They were due to spend the night and Christmas day at the Vance house. As they walked swiftly along with the elastic tread of youth, they simultaneously halted before the blind musician and pressed into his trembling hand a bountiful gift; then they hurried away to escape his thanks.

At the hotel Livingston called for a private dining room, and after the coffee was served, he said:

"Tell me, Briggs, what is the link between you and your patient. There is a link, I am sure. Her words while in the trance made a great impression upon me."

There was a pause before Reuel replied in a low tone, as he rested his arm on the opposite side of the table and propped his head up on his hand:

"Forgive me, Aubrey!"

"For what?"

"This playing with your confidence. I have not been entirely frank with you."

"Oh, well! you are not bound to tell me everything you know. You surely have the right to silence about your affairs, if you think best."

"Listen, Aubrey. I should like to tell you all about it. I would feel better. What you say is true; there is a link; but I never saw her in the flesh before that night at the Temple. With all our knowledge, Aubrey, we are but barbarians in our ideas of the beginning, interim and end of our creation. Why were we created? for whose benefit? can anyone answer that satisfactorily?

" 'Few things are hidden from the man who devotes himself earnestly and servicously to the solution of a mystery,' Hawthorne tells us," replied Aubrey. "Have not you proved this, Reuel?"

"Well, yes—or, we prove rather, that our solution but deepens the mystery of mysteries. I have surely proved the last. Aubrey, I look natural, don't I? There is nothing about me that seems wrong?"

"Wrong! No."

"Well, if I tell you the truth you will call me a lunatic. You have heard of people being haunted by hallucinations?" Aubrey nodded. "I am one of those persons. Seven weeks ago I saw Dianthe first, but not in the flesh. Hallow-eve I spoke to her in the garden of the haunted house, but not in the flesh. I thought it strange to be sure, that this face should lurk in my mind so much of the time; but I never dreamed what a crisis it was leading up to. The French and German schools of philosophy have taught us that going to places and familiar passages in books, of which we have had no previous knowledge, is but a proof of Plato's doctrine—the soul's transmigration, and reflections from the invisible world surrounding us.

"Finally a mad desire seized me to find that face a living

reality that I might love and worship it. Then I saw her at the Temple—I found her at the hospital—*in the flesh*! My desire was realized."

"And having found her, what then?" He waited breathlessly for the reply.

"I am mightily pleased and satisfied. I will cure her. She is charming; and if it is insanity to be in love with her, I don't care to be sane."

Livingston did not reply at once. His face was like marble in its impassiveness. The other's soft tremulous tones, fearless yet moist eyes and broken sentences, appeared to awaken no response in his breast. Instead, a far-off gleam came into his blue eyes. At last he broke the silence with the words:

"You name it well; it is insanity indeed, for you to love this woman."

"Why?" asked his friend, constrainedly.

"Because it is not for the best."

"For her or me?"

"Oh, for *her*—" he finished the sentence with an expressive gesture.

"I understand you, Aubrey. I should not have believed it of you. If it were one of the other fellows; but you are generally so charitable."

"You forget your own words: 'Tramps, stray dogs and Negroes—,'" he quoted significantly. "Then there is your professional career to be considered,—you mean honorable, do you not?— How can you succeed if it be hinted abroad that you are married to a Negress?"

"I have thought of all that. I am determined. I will marry her in spite of hell itself! Marry her before she awakens to consciousness of her identity. I'm not unselfish; I don't pretend to be. There is no sin in taking her out of the sphere where she was born. God and science helping me, I will give her life and love and wifehood and maternity and perfect health. God, Aubrey! you, with all you have had of life's sweetness, petted idol of a beautiful world, you who will soon feel the heart-beats of your wife against your breast when lovely Molly is eternally bound to you, what do you know of a lonely, darkened life like mine? I have not the manner nor the charm which wins women. Men like me get love from them which is half akin to pity, when they get anything at all. It is but the shadow. This is my opportunity for happiness; I seize it. Fate has linked us together and no man and no man's laws shall part us."

Livingston sipped his wine quietly, intently watching Reuel's face. Now he leaned across the table and stretched out his hand to Briggs; his eyes looked full into his. As their hands met in a close clasp, he whispered a sentence across the board. Reuel started, uttered an exclamation and flushed slowly a dark, dull red.

"How—where—how did you know it?" he stammered.

"I have known it since first we met; but the secret is safe with me."

CHAPTER VI

HE scene which met the gaze when an hour later the young men were ushered into the long drawing-room of the Vance house was one well-calculated to remove all gloomy, pessimistic reasoning. Warmth, gaiety, pretty women, luxury,—all sent the blood leaping through the veins in delightful anticipation.

Their entrance was greeted by a shout of welcome.

"Oh, Aubrey! I am so glad you are come," cried Molly from the far end of the room. "Fancy tomorrow being Christmas! Shall we be ready for all that company tomorrow night and the ballroom, dining room and hall yet to be trimmed? Is it possible to be ready?"

"Not if we stand dwadling in idle talk." This from "Adonis," who was stretched full length on the sitting-room sofa, with a cigarette between his lips, his hands under his handsome head, surrounded by a bevy of pretty, chattering girls, prominent among whom was Cora Scott, who aided and abetted Charlie in every piece of mischief.

Molly curled her lip but deigned no reply.

Bert Smith, from a corner of the room where he was about ascending a step-ladder, flung a book heavily at Adonis's lazy figure.

"Don't confuse your verbs," exclaimed Aubrey. "How can you stand when you are lying down, and were you ever known to do anything else but dwadle, Adonis—eh?"

"I give it up," said Charlie, sleepily, kicking the book off the sofa.

"Is this an amateur grocery shop, may I ask, Miss Vance?" continued Aubrey as he and Briggs made their way to their hostess through an avalanche of parcels and baskets strewn on the tables and the floor.

Molly laughed as she greeted them. "No wonder you are surprised. I am superintending the arrangement of my poor people's gifts," she explained. "They must all be sent out tonight. I don't know what I should have done without all these good people to help me. But there are *piles* to be done yet. There is the tree, the charades, etc., etc.," she continued, in a plaintive little voice.

"More particularly cetra, cetra," said Aubrey from Bert's corner where he had gone to help along the good works of placing holly wreaths.

"Oh, you, Aubrey—stop being a magpie." Aubrey and Molly were very matter of fact lovers.

"Molly," again broke in Charlie, "suppose the box from Pierson's has never come, won't you be up a tree?" and the speaker opened his handsome eyes wide, and shook off his cigarette-ash.

Molly maintained a dignified silence toward her brother. The firelight danced and dwelt upon her lovingly. She was so pretty, so fair, so slender, so graceful. Now in her gray plush tea-gown, with her hair piled picturesquely on the top of her small head, and fixed there with a big tortoise-shell pin, it would have been difficult to find a more delightful object for the gaze to rest upon.

"We shall have to fall back upon the wardrobes," she said at length. "You are a horrid wet-blanket, Charlie! I am sure I—"

Her remarks were cut short as the door opened, and with laughter and shouting a bevy of young people who had been at work in another part of the house rushed in. "It is come; it's all right; don't worry, Molly!" they sang in chorus.

"Do be quiet all of you; one can hardly hear oneself speak!"

The box from the costumer's had arrived; the great costume party was saved; in short, excitement and bustle were in full swing at Vance Hall as it had been at Christmas-time since the young people could remember.

Adonis lifted himself from the sofa and proposed to open the box of dresses at once, and try them on.

"Charlie, you are a brick!—the very thing!"

"Oh! yes, yes; let us try them on!"

Molly broke through the eager voices: "And we have not done the ball-room yet!" she said reproachfully.

"Oh! bother the ball-room!" declared Adonis, now thoroughly aroused. "We have all night. We can't do better than to don our finery."

Molly sat down with an air of resigned patience. "I promised Mr. Pierson," she observed quietly, "that the box should not be touched until he was here to superintend matters."

"Oh, Pierson be blowed!" elegantly observed her brother. But Reuel Briggs suddenly dropped his work, walked over, and sided with Molly.

"You are quite right, Miss Molly; and you Charlie and Aubrey and the rest of you men, if you want to open the box tonight you must first decorate the ball-room. Business before pleasure."

"Saved!—saved! See my brave, true knight defends his lady fair." Molly danced, practising the step she was about to astonish the company with on Christmas-night. "I think I am what the Scotch call 'fev,'" she laughed. "I don't know why I feel so awfully jolly tonight. I could positively fly from sheer excitement and delight."

"Don't you know why?" observed Cora. "I will tell you. It is because this is your last Christmas as Molly Vance; next year—"

"Ah, do not!" interrupted Molly, quickly. "Who knows what a year may bring forth. Is it not so, Dr. Briggs?" she turned appealingly to Reuel.

"Grief follows joy as clouds the sunlight. 'Woe! woe! each heart must bleed, must break,'" was his secret thought as he bowed gravely. But on his face was a look of startled perplexity, for suddenly as she spoke to him it appeared that a dark veil settled like a pall over the laughing face at his side. He shivered.

"What's the matter, Briggs!" called out Adonis. They had reached the ball-room and were standing over the piles of holly and evergreen, ready for an onslaught on the walls.

"Don't be surprised if Briggs acts strangely," continued Charlie. "It is in order for him to whoop it up in the spirit line."

"Why, Charlie! What do you mean?" questioned Molly with an anxious glance at Reuel.

"Anything interesting, Charlie?" called out a jolly girl across the room.

"Briggs is our 'show' man. Haven't you heard, girls, what a celebrity is with you tonight? Briggs is a philosopher—mesmerism is his specialty. Say, old man, give the company a specimen of your infernal art, can't you? He goes the whole hog, girls; can even raise the dead."

"Let up, Charlie," said Aubrey in a low tone. "It's no joking matter."

There were screams and exclamations from the girls. With reckless gaiety Adonis continued,

"What is to be the outcome of the great furore you have created, Briggs?"

"Nothing of moment, I hope," smiled Reuel, good-naturedly. "I have been simply an instrument; I leave results to the good angels who direct events. What does Longfellow say about the arrow and the song?

> *'Long, long afterwards, in an oak*
> *I found the arrow still unbroke;*
> *And the song, from beginning to end,*
> *I found in the heart of a friend.'*

May it be so with my feeble efforts."

"But circumstances alter cases. In this case, the 'arrow' is a girl and a devilish handsome one, too; and the 'air' is the whole scientific world. Your philosophy and mysticism gave way before Beauty. Argument is a stubborn man's castle, but the heart is still unconvinced."

" 'I mixed those children up, and not a creature knew it,' " hummed Bert Smith. "Your ideas are mixed, Don; stick to the ladies, you understand girls and horseflesh: philosophy isn't in your line."

"Oh, sure!" said Adonis unruffled by his friend's words.

"Charlie Vance," said Molly severely, "if we have any more *swearing* from you tonight, you leave the room until you learn to practice good manners. I'm surprised at your language!"

"Just the same, Briggs is a fraud. I shall keep my eye on him. It's a case of beauty and the beast. Oh," he continued in malicious glee, "wouldn't you girls turn green with envy, every man jack of you, if you could see the beauty!"

Thereupon the girls fell to pelting him with holly wreaths and evergreen festoons, much to the enjoyment of Mr. Vance, who had entered unperceived in the general melee.

"What is it all about, Dr. Briggs?" asked Molly in a low voice.

"It is the case of a patient who was in a mesmeric sleep and

I was fortunate enough to awaken her. She is a waif; and it will be months before she will be well and strong, poor girl."

"Do you make a study of mesmerism, Doctor?" asked Mr. Vance from his armchair by the glowing fire.

"Yes sir; and a wonderful science it is." Before Mr. Vance could continue, Livingston said: "If you folks will be still for about ten minutes, I'll tell you what happened in my father's house when I was a very small boy; I can just remember it."

"If it's a ghost story, make it strong, Aubrey, so that not a girl will sleep tonight. Won't the dears look pretty blinking and yawning tomorrow night? We'll hear 'em, fellows, in the small hours of the morning, 'Molly, Molly! I'm so frightened. I do believe someone is in my room: may I come in with you, dear?'"

"Charlie, stop your nonsense," laughed his father, and Adonis obediently subsided.

"My father was Dr. Aubrey Livingston too," began Aubrey, "and he owned a large plantation of slaves. My father was deeply interested in the science of medicine, and I believe made some valuable discoveries along the line of mesmeric phenomena, for some two or three of his books are referred to even at this advanced stage of discovery, as marvellous in some of their data.

"Among the slaves was a girl who was my mother's waiting maid, and I have seen my father throw her into a trance-state many times when I was so small that I had no conception of what he was doing.

"Many a time I have known him to call her into the parlor to perform tricks of mind-reading for the amusement of visitors, and many wonderful things were done by her as the record given in his books shows.

"One day there was a great dinner party given at our place, and the elite of the county were bidden. It was about two years before the civil war, and our people were not expecting war;

thinking that all unpleasantness must end in their favor, they gave little heed to the ominous rumble of public opinion that was arising at the North, but went on their way in all their pride of position and wealth without a care for the future.

"Child as I was I was impressed by the beauty and wit of the women and the chivalric bearing of the men gathered about my father's hospitable board on that memorable day. When the feasting and mirth began to lag, someone called for Mira—the maid—and my father sent for her to come and amuse the guests.

"My father made the necessary passes and from a serious, rather sad Negress, very mild with everyone, Mira changed to a gay, noisy, restless woman, full of irony and sharp jesting. In this case this peculiar metamorphosis always occurred. Nothing could be more curious than to see her and hear her. 'Tell the company what you see, Mira,' commanded my father.

"You will not like it, captain; but if I must, I must. All the women will be widows and the men shall sleep in early graves. They come from the north, from the east, from the west, they sweep to the gulf through a trail of blood. Your houses shall burn, your fields be laid waste, and a downtrodden race shall rule in your land. For you, captain, a prison cell and a pauper's grave."

The dinner-party broke up in a panic, and from that time my father could not abide the girl. He finally sold her just a few months before the secession of the Confederate States, and that was the last we ever knew of her."

"And did the prophecy come true about your father?" asked Mr. Vance.

"Too true, sir; my father died while held as a prisoner of war, in Boston Harbor. And every woman at the table was left a widow. There is only too much truth in science of mesmeric phenomena. The world is a wonderful place."

"Wonderful!" declared his hearers.

"I am thinking of that poor, pretty creature living ill in that gloomy hospital without a friend. Men are selfish! I tell you what, folks, tomorrow after lunch we'll make a Christmas visit to the patients, and carry them fruit and flowers. As for your beautiful patient, Dr. Briggs, she shall not be friendless any longer, she shall come to us at Vance Hall."

"Molly!" broke simultaneously from Aubrey and Charlie.

"Oh, I mean it. There is plenty of room in this great house, and here she shall remain until she is restored to health."

Expostulation was in vain. The petted heiress was determined, and when Mr. Vance was appealed to he laughed and said, as he patted her hand:

"The queen must have her own."

At length the costumer's box was opened amidst jest, song and laughter. The characters were distributed by the wilful Molly. Thus attired, to the music of Tannhauser's march, played by one of the girls on the piano, the gay crowd marched and counter-marched about the spacious room.

In the early morning hours, Aubrey Livingston slept and dreamed of Dianthe Lusk, and these words haunted his sleep and lingered with him when he woke:

"She had the glory of heaven in her voice, and in her face the fatal beauty of man's terrible sins."

Aubrey Livingston knew that he was hopelessly lost as was Adam when he sold his heavenly birthright for a woman's smile.

CHAPTER VII

HROUGH days and days, and again through days and days, over and over again, Reuel Briggs fought to restore his patient to a normal condition of health. Physically, he succeeded; but mentally his treatment was a failure. Memory remained a blank to the unhappy girl. Her life virtually began with her awakening at the hospital. A look of wonder and a faint smile were the only replies that questions as to the past elicited from her. Old and tried specialists in brain diseases and hypnotic states came from every part of the Union on bootless errands. It was decided that nothing could be done; rest, freedom from every care and time might eventually restore the poor, violated mind to its original strength. Thus it was that Dianthe became the dear adopted daughter of the medical profession. Strange to say, Molly Vance secured her desire, and wearing the name of Felice Adams, Dianthe was domiciled under the roof of palatial Vance hall, and the small annuity provided by the generous contributions of the physicians of the country was placed in the hands of Mr. Vance, Sr., to be expended for their protege.

The astonishing nature of the startling problems he had unearthed, the agitation and indignation aroused in him by the heartless usage to which his patient must have been exposed, haunted Briggs day and night. He believed that he had been drawn into active service for Dianthe by a series of strange coincidences, and the subtle forces of immortality; what future acts this service might require he knew not, he cared not; he registered a solemn promise to perform all tasks allotted him by Infinity, to the fullest extent of his power.

The brilliant winter days merged themselves into spring. After one look into Dianthe's eyes, so deep, clear and true, Molly Vance had surrendered unconditionally to the charm of the beautiful stranger, drawn by an irresistible bond of sympathy. "Who would believe," she observed to Livingston, "that at this stage of the world's progress one's identity could be so easily lost and one still be living. It is like a page from an exciting novel."

With the impulsiveness of youth, a wonderful friendship sprang up between the two; they rode, walked and shopped together; in short, became inseparable companions. The stranger received every attention in the family that could be given an honored guest. Livingston and Briggs watched her with some anxiety; would she be able to sustain the position of intimate friendship to which Molly had elected her? But both breathed more freely when they noted her perfect manners, the ease and good-breeding displayed in all her intercourse with those socially above the level to which they knew this girl was born. She accepted the luxury of her new surroundings as one to the manner born.

"We need not have feared for her; by Jove, she's a thorough-bred!" exclaimed Aubrey one day to Reuel. The latter nodded as he looked up from his book.

"And why not? Probably the best blood of the country flows in the poor girl's veins. Who can tell? Why should she not be a thorough-bred."

"True," replied Aubrey, as a slight frown passed over his face.

"I am haunted by a possibility, Aubrey," continued Reuel. "What if memory suddenly returns? Is it safe to risk the

unpleasantness of a public reawakening of her sleeping faculties? I have read of such things."

Aubrey shrugged his handsome shoulders. "We must risk
something for the sake of science; where no one is injured by
deception there is no harm done."

"Now that question has presented itself to me repeatedly
lately: Is deception justifiable for any reason? Somehow it
haunts me that trouble may come from this. I wish we had told
the exact truth about her identity."

" 'If 'twere done when 'tis done, then 'twere well it were
done quickly" murmured Aubrey with a sarcastic smile on his
face. "How you balk at nothing, Reuel," he drawled mockingly.

"Oh, call me a fool and done with it, Aubrey: I suppose I am;
but one didn't make one's self."

Drives about the snow-clad suburbs of Cambridge with
Briggs and Molly, at first helped to brighten the invalid; then came
quiet social diversions at which Dianthe was the great attraction.

It was at an afternoon function that Reuel took courage to
speak of his love. A dozen men buzzed about "Miss Adams" in
the great bay window where Molly had placed Dianthe, her
superb beauty set off by a simple toilet. People came and went
constantly. Musical girls, generally with gold eyeglasses on aes-
thetic noses, played grim classical preparations, which have as
cheerful an effect on a gay crowd as the perfect, irreproachable
skeleton of a bygone beauty might have; or articulate, with cultivation and no voices to speak of, arias which would sap the life
of a true child of song to render as the maestro intended.

The grand, majestic voice that had charmed the hearts from
thousands of bosoms, was pinioned in the girl's throat like an
imprisoned song-bird. Dianthe's voice was completely gone
along with her memory. But music affected her strangely, and
Reuel watched her anxiously.

Her face was a study in its delicate, quickly changing tints, its sparkle of smiles running from the sweet, pure tremor of the lovely mouth to the swift laughter of eyes and voice.

Mindful of her infirmity, Reuel led her to the conservatory to escape the music. She lifted her eyes to his with a curious and angelic light in them. She was conscious that he loved her with his whole most loving heart. She winced under the knowledge, for while she believed in him, depended upon him and gathered strength from his love, what she gave in return was but a slight, cold affection compared with his adoration.

He brought her refreshments in the conservatory, and then told his love and asked his fate. She did not answer at once, but looked at his plain face, at the stalwart elegance of his figure, and again gazed into the dark, true, clever eyes, and with the sigh of a tired child crept into his arms, and into his heart for all time and eternity. Thus Aubrey Livingston found them when the company had departed. So it was decided to have the wedding in June. What need for these two children of misfortune to wait?

Briggs, with his new interest in life, felt that it was good just to be alive. The winter passed rapidly, and as he threaded the streets coming and going to his hospital duties, his heart sang. No work was now too arduous; he delighted in the duty most exacting in its nature. As the spring came in it brought with it thoughts of the future. He was almost penniless, and he saw no way of obtaining the money he needed. He had not been improvident, but his lonely life had lived a reckless disregard of the future, and the value of money. He often lived a day on bread and water, at the same time sitting without a fire in the coldest weather because his pockets were empty and he was too proud to ask a loan, or solicit credit from storekeepers. He now found himself in great difficulty. His literary work and the extra cases which his recent triumph had brought him, barely sufficed for his own present needs. Alone in his bachelor existence he would call this luxury, but it was not enough to furnish a suitable establishment for Dianthe. As the weeks rolled by and nothing presented itself, he grew anxious, and finally resolved to consult Livingston.

All things had become new to him, and in the light of his great happiness the very face of old Cambridge was changed. Fate had always been against him, and had played him the shabbiest of tricks, but now he felt that she might do her worst, he held a talisman against misfortune while his love remained to him. Thinking thus he walked along briskly, and the sharp wind brought a faint color into his sallow face. He tried to think and plan, but his ideas were whirled away before they had taken form, and he felt a giant's power to overcome with each inspiring breath of the crisp, cool March air. Aubrey should plan for him, but he would accomplish.

Livingston had apartments on Dana Hill, the most aristocratic portion of Cambridge. There he would remain till the autumn, when he would marry Molly Vance, and remove to Virginia and renew the ancient splendor of his ancestral home. He was just dressing for an evening at the theatre when Briggs entered his rooms. He greeted him with his usual genial warmth.

"What!" he said gaily, "the great scientist here, at this hour?" Then noticing his visitor's anxious countenance he added: "What's the matter?"

"I am in difficulties and come to you for help," replied Reuel.

"How so? What is it? I am always anxious to serve you, Briggs."

"I certainly think so or I would not be here now," said Reuel. "But you are just going out, an engagement perhaps with Miss Molly. My business will take some time—"

Aubrey interrupted him, shaking his head negatively, "I was only going out to wile away the time at the theatre. Sit down and free your mind, old man."

Thus admonished, Reuel flung himself among the cushions of the divan, and began to state his reasons for desiring assistance: when he finished, Livingston asked:

"Has nothing presented itself?"

"O yes; two or three really desirable offers which I wrote to accept, but to my surprise, in each case I received polite regrets that circumstances had arisen to prevent the acceptance of my valuable services. That is what puzzles me. What the dickens did it mean?"

Aubrey said nothing but continued a drum solo on the arm of his chair. Finally he asked abruptly: "Briggs, do you think anyone knows or suspects your origin?"

Not a muscle of Reuel's face moved as he replied, calmly: "I have been wondering if such can be the case."

"This infernal prejudice is something horrible. It closes the door of hope and opportunity in many a good man's face. I am a Southerner, but I am ashamed of my section," he added warmly.

Briggs said nothing, but a dark, dull red spread slowly to the very roots of his hair. Presently Aubrey broke the painful silence.

"Briggs, I think I can help you."

"How?"

"There's an expedition just about starting from England for Africa; its final destination is, I believe, the site of ancient Ethiopian cities; its object to unearth buried cities and treasure which the shifting sands of Sahara have buried for centuries. This expedition lacks just such a medical man as you; the salary is large, but you must sign for two years; that is my reason for not mentioning it before. It bids fair to be a wonderful venture and there will be plenty of glory for those who return, beside the good it will do to the Negro race if it proves the success in discovery that scholars predict. I don't advise you to even consider this opportunity, but you asked for my help and this is all I can offer at present."

"But Dianthe!" exclaimed Reuel faintly.

"Yes," smiled Aubrey. "Don't I know how I would feel if it were Molly and I was in your place? You are like all other men, Reuel. Passion does not calculate, and therein lies its strength. As long as common sense lasts we are not in love. Now the answer to the question of ways and means is with you; it is in your hands. You will choose love and poverty I suppose; I should. There are people fools enough to tell a man in love to keep cool. Bah! It is an impossible thing."

"Does true love destroy our reasoning faculties?" Reuel asked himself as he sat there in silence after his friend ceased speaking. He felt then that he could not accept this offer. Finally he got upon his feet, still preserving his silence, and made ready to leave his friend. When he reached the door, he turned and said: "I will see you in the morning."

For a long time after Briggs had gone, Aubrey sat smoking and gazing into the glowing coals that filled the open grate.

All that night Reuel remained seated in his chair or pacing the cheerless room, conning ways and means to extricate himself from his dilemma without having recourse to the last extremity proposed by Aubrey. It was a brilliant opening; there was no doubt of that; a year—six months ago—he would have hailed it with delight, but if he accepted it, it would raise a barrier between his love and him which could not be overcome—the ocean and thousands of miles.

"Oh, no!" he cried, "a thousand times no! Rather give up my ambitions."

Then growing more rational he gazed mournfully around the poor room and asked himself if he could remain and see his wife amid such surroundings? That would be impossible. The question then, resolved itself into two parts: If he remained at home, they could not marry, therefore separation; if he went abroad, marriage and separation. He caught at the last thought eagerly. If then they were doomed to separate, of two evils why not choose the least? The African position would at least bind them irrevocably together. Instantly hope resumed its sway in Reuel's breast so fertile is the human mind in expedients to calm the ruffled spirit; he began to estimate the advantages he would gain by accepting the position: He could marry Dianthe, settle a large portion of his salary upon her thus rendering her independent of charity, leave her in the care of the Vance family, and return in two years a wealthy man no longer fearing poverty. He had never before built golden castles, but now he speculated upon the possibility of unearthing gems and gold from the mines of ancient Meroe and the pyramids of Ethiopia. In the midst of his fancies he fell asleep. In the morning he felt a wonderful relief as he contemplated his decision. Peace had returned to his mind. He determined to see Aubrey at once and learn all the particulars concerning the expedition. Providentially, Aubrey was just sitting down to breakfast and over a cup of steaming coffee Reuel told his decision, ending with these words: "Now, my dear Aubrey, it may be the last request I may ever ask of you, for who can tell what strange adventures may await me in that dark and unknown country to which Fate has doomed me?"

Livingston tried to remonstrate with him.

"I know what I am saying. The climate is murderous, to begin with, and there are many other dangers. It is better to be prepared. I have no friend but you."

"Between us, Reuel, oaths are useless; you may count upon my loyalty to all your interests," said Aubrey with impressiveness.

"I shall ask you to watch over Dianthe. I intrust her to you as I would intrust her to my brother, had I one. This is all I ask of you when I am in that far country."

With open brow, clear eyes and grave face, Aubrey Livingston replied in solemn tones:

"Reuel, you may sail without a fear. Molly and I will have her with us always like a dear sister."

Hand clasped in hand they stood a moment as if imploring heaven's blessing on the solemn compact. Then they turned the conversation on the business of securing the position at once.

CHAPTER VIII

EUEL was greatly touched during the next three months by the devotion of his friend Livingston, whose unselfishness in his behalf he had before had cause to notice. Nor was this all; he seemed capable of any personal sacrifice that the welfare of Briggs demanded.

Before many days had passed he had placed the young man in direct communication with the English officials in charge of the African expedition. The salary was most generous; in fact, all the arrangements were highly satisfactory. Whatever difficulties really existed melted, as it were, before Aubrey's influence, and Reuel would have approached the time of departure over a bed of roses but for the pain of parting with Dianthe.

At length the bustle of graduation was over. The last article of the traveler's outfit was bought. The morning of the day of departure was to see the ceremony performed that would unite the young people for life. It was a great comfort to Reuel that Charlie Vance had decided to join the party as a tourist for the sake of the advantages of such a trip.

The night before their departure Aubrey Livingston entertained the young men at dinner in his rooms along with a number of college professors and other learned savans. The most complimentary things were said of Reuel in the after-dinner toasts, the best of wishes were uttered together with congratulations on the marriage of the morrow for they all admired the young enthusiast. His superiority was so evident that none disputed it; they envied him, but were not jealous. The object of their felicitations smiled seldom.

"Come, for heaven sake shake off your sadness; be the happy groom upon whom Fortune, fickle jade, has at last consented to smile," cried Adonis. So, amid laughter and jest, the night passed and the morrow came.

After his guests had departed, Aubrey Livingston went to the telegraph office and sent a message:

"To Jim Titus,

> "*Laurel Hill, Virginia:—*
>
> "*Be on hand at the New York dock, Trans-Atlantic Steamship Co., on the first. I will be there to make things right for you. Ten thousand if you succeed the first six months.*
>
> *A.L.*"

*   *   *   *   *

It was noon the next day and the newly wedded stood with clasped hands uttering their good-byes.

"You must not be unhappy, dear. The time will run by before you know it, and I shall be with you again. Meanwhile there is plenty to occupy you. You have Molly and Aubrey to take you about. But pray remember my advice,—don't attempt too much; you're not strong by any means."

"No, I am not strong!" she interrupted with a wild burst of tears. "Reuel, if you knew how weak I am you would not leave me."

Her husband drew the fair head to his bosom, pressing back the thick locks with a lingering lover's touch.

"I wish to God I could take you with me," he said tenderly after a silence. "Dear girl, you know this grief of yours would break my heart, only that it shows how well you love me. I am proud of every tear." She looked at him with an expression he could not read; it was full of unutterable emotion—love, anguish, compassion.

"Oh," she said passionately, "nothing remains long with us but sorrow and regret. Every good thing may be gone tomorrow—lost! Do you know, I sometimes dream or have waking visions of a past time in my life? But when I try to grasp the fleeting memories they leave me groping in darkness. Can't you help me, Reuel?"

With a laugh he kissed away her anxieties, although he was dismayed to know that at most any time full memory might return. He must speak to Aubrey. Then he closed her lips with warm lingering kisses.

"Be a good girl and pray for your husband's safety, that God may let us meet again and be happy! Don't get excited. That you *must* guard against."

And Reuel Briggs, though his eyes were clouded with tears, was a happy man at heart that day. Just that once he tasted to the full all that there is of happiness in human life. Happy is he who is blessed with even *one* perfect day in a lifetime of sorrow. His last memory of her was a mute kiss and low "God bless you," broken by a sob. And so they parted.

In the hall below Molly Vance met him with a sisterly kiss for good-bye; outside in the carriage sat Mr. Vance, Sr., Charlie and Aubrey waiting to drive to the depot.

*   *   *   *   *

Reuel Briggs, Charlie Vance and their servant, Jim Titus, sailed from New York for Liverpool, England, on the first day of July.

*   *   *   *   *

The departure of the young men made a perceptible break in the social circle at Vance Hall. Mr. Vance buried himself in the details of business and the two girls wandered disconsolately about the house and grounds attended by Livingston, who was at the Hall constantly and pursued them with delicate attentions.

By common consent it was determined that no summer exodus could be thought of until after the travellers had reached August, all being well, they would seek the limit of civilized intercourse in Africa. While waiting, to raise the spirits of the family, it was decided to invite a house party for the remainder of July, and in the beauties of Bar Harbor. Soon gaiety and laughter filled the grand old rooms; the days went merrily by.

Two men were sitting in the billiard room lounging over iced punch. Light, perfumed and golden, poured from the rooms below upon the summer night, and the music of a waltz made its way into the darkness.

"What an odd fish Livingston has grown to be," said one, relighting a thin, delicate-looking cigar. "I watched him out of curiosity a while ago and was struck at the change in him."

"Ah!" drawled the other sipping the cooling beverage. "Quite a Priuli on the whole, eh?"

"Y-e-s! Precisely. And I have fancied that the beautiful Mrs. Briggs is his Clarisse. What do you think? She shudders every time he draws near, and sinks to the ground under the steady gaze of his eye. Odd, isn't it?"

"Deucedly odd! About to marry Miss Vance, isn't he?"

"That don't count. Love is not always legitimate. If there's anything in it, it is only a flirtation probably; that's the style."

"What you say is true, Skelton. Let's drink the rest of this stuff and go down again. I know we're missed already."

When they had swallowed the punch and descended, the first person they saw was Livingston leaning against the door of the salon. His face was abstracted and in dead repose, there lurked about the corners of his full lips implacable resolution. The waltz was ended.

Some interminable argument was going on, generally, about

the room. Conversation progressed in sharp, brisk sentences, which fell from the lips like the dropping shots of sharpshooters. There was a call for music. Molly mentally calculated her available talent and was about to give up the idea and propose something else, when she was amazed to see Dianthe rise hurriedly from her seat on an ottoman, go to the piano unattended and sit down. Unable to move with astonishment she watched in fascination the slender white fingers flash over the keys. There was a strange rigid appearance about the girl that was unearthly. Never once did she raise her eyes. At the first sharp treble note the buzz in the room was hushed at stillness. Livingston moved forward and rested his arm upon the piano fastening his gaze upon the singer's quivering lips.

Slowly, tremulously at first, pealed forth the notes:

"Go down, Moses, way down in Egypt's land,

Tell ol' Pharaoh, let my people go."

Scarcely was the verse begun when every person in the room started suddenly and listened with eager interest. As the air proceeded, some grew visibly pale, and not daring to breathe a syllable, looked horrified into each other's faces. "Great heaven!" whispered Mr. Vance to his daughter, "do you not hear another voice beside Mrs. Briggs'?"

It was true, indeed. A weird contralto, veiled as it were, rising and falling upon every wave of the great soprano, and reaching the ear as from some strange distance. The singer sang on, her voice dropping sweet and low, the echo following it, and at the closing word, she fell back in a dead faint. Mr. Vance caught her in his arms.

"Mrs. Briggs has the soul of an artiste. She would make a perfect prima donna for the Grand Opera," remarked one man to Molly.

"We are as surprised as anyone," replied the young girl; "we never knew that Mrs. Briggs was musical until this evening. It is a delightful surprise."

They carried her to the quiet, cool library away from the glaring lights and the excitement, and at her request left her there alone. Her thoughts were painful. Memory had returned in full save as to her name. She knit her brow in painful thought, finally leaning back among her cushions wearily, too puzzled for further thought. Presently a step paused beside her chair. She looked up into Livingston's face.

"Are you feeling better?" he asked, gently taking in her slender wrist and counting the pulse-beats.

Instead of answering his question, she began abruptly: "Mr. Livingston, Reuel told me to trust you implicitly. Can you and will you tell me what has happened to me since last I sang the song I have sung here tonight? I try to recall the past, but all is confusion and mystery. It makes my head ache so to think."

Livingston suddenly drew closer to her.

"Yes, Felice, there *is* a story in your life! I can save you."

"Save me!" exclaimed the girl.

"Yes, and will! Listen to me." In gentle accents he recounted to her there in the stillness, with the pulsing music of the viols beating and throbbing in her ears like muffled drums, the story of Dianthe Lusk as we have told it here. At the close of the tale the white-faced girl turned to him in despair the more eloquent because of her quietness.

"Did Reuel know that I was a Negress?"

"No; no one recognized you but myself."

She hid her face in her hands.

"Who ever suffered such torture as mine?" she cried, bitterly. "And there is no rest out of the grave!" she continued.

"Yes, there is rest and security in my love! Felice, Dianthe, I have learned to love you!"

She sprang from his touch as if stung.

He continued: "I love you better than all in the world. To possess you I am prepared to save you from the fate that must be yours if ever Reuel learns your origin."

"You would have me give up all for you?" she asked with a shudder.

"Ay, from your husband—from the world! We will go where none can ever find us. If you refuse, I cannot aid you."

"Pity me!"

She sank upon her knees at his feet.

"I give you a week to think it over. I can love, but cannot pity."

In vain the girl sought to throw off the numbing influence of the man's presence. In desperation she tried to defy him, but she knew that she had lost her will-power and was but a puppet in the hands of this false friend.

CHAPTER IX

"THE Doctor is so good to you about letters; so different from poor Charlie. I can't imagine what he finds to write about."

It was the first of August, and the last guest had left the mansion; tomorrow they started for Bar Harbor. Molly, Dianthe and Livingston sat together in the morning room.

"He tells me the incidents of the journey. This is the last letter for three months," said Dianthe, with a sigh.

"Of course, there is no love-making," said Aubrey, lazily letting fall his newspaper, and pushing his hands through his bright hair. He was a sight for gods and men. His handsome figure outlined against the sky, as he stood by the window in an attitude of listless grace, his finely-cut face, so rich in color and the charm of varying expression, turned indolently toward the two women to whom the morning mail had brought its offering.

"Have you ever read one of Reuel's letters?" Dianthe said, quietly. "You may see this if you like." A tap sounded on the door.

"Miss Molly, if you please, the dressmaker has sent the things."

"Oh, thank you, Jennie, I'll come at once!" and gathering up her letters, Molly ran off with a smile and a nod of apology.

Aubrey stood by the window reading Reuel's letter. His face was deadly white, and his breath came quick and short. He read half the page; then crushed it in his hand and crossed the room to Dianthe. She, too, was pale and there was something akin to fear in the gaze that she lifted to his face.

"How dare you?" he asked breathlessly; "but you are a woman! Not one of you has any delicacy in her heart! Not one!"

He tore the letter across and flung it from him.

"I do not suffer enough," he said in a suffocated voice. "You taunt me with this view of conjugal happiness—with his *right* to love and care for you."

"I did not do it to hurt you," she answered. "Do you have no thought for Molly's sufferings if I succumb to your threats of exposure and weakly allow myself to be frightened into committing the great wrong you contemplate toward two true-hearted people? I thought you could realize if you could *know* how Reuel loves and trusts me, and how true and noble is his nature."

"Do you think I have room to pity Reuel—Molly—while my own pain is more than I can bear? Without you my ambition is destroyed, my hope for the future—my life is ruined."

He turned from her and going to a distant part of the room, threw himself into a chair and covered his face with his hands. Against her will, better promptings and desires, the unfortunate girl is drawn by invisible influences across the room to the man's side. Presently he holds her in his eager, strong embrace, his face and tears hidden against her shoulder. She does not struggle in his clasp, only looks into the future with the hopeless agony of dumb despair.

At length he broke the silence. "There is nothing you can feel, or say to me that I do not realize—the sin, the shame, the lasting disgrace. I know it all. I told you once I loved you; I tell you now that I cannot *live* without you!"

An hour later Dianthe sat alone in the pleasant room. She did not realize the beauty of the languid mid-summer day. She thought of nothing but the wickedness of betraying her friends. Her perfect features were like marble. The dark eyes had deep, black circles round them and gazed wistfully into the far, far distance, a land where spirit only could compass the wide space. As she sat there in full possession of all her waking faculties, suddenly there rose from out the very floor, as it were, a pale and lovely woman. She neither looked at Dianthe nor did she speak; but walked to the table and opened a book lying upon it and wrote; then coming back, stood for a moment fixed; then sank, just as she rose, and disappeared. Her dress was that of a servant. Her head was bare; her hair fell loosely around her in long black curls. Her complexion was the olive of mulattoes or foreigners. As the woman passed from her view, Dianthe rose and went to the table to examine the book. She did not feel at all frightened, recognizing instantly the hand of mysticism in this strange occurrence. There on the open page, she perceived heavy marks in ink, under-scoring the following quotation from the twelfth chapter of Luke: "For there is nothing covered that shall not be revealed." On the margin, at the end of this passage was written in a fine female hand, the single word, "Mira."

$$* \quad * \quad * \quad * \quad *$$

After luncheon Aubrey proposed that they go canoeing on the river. The idea was eagerly embraced and by five o'clock the large and luxurious canoe floated out from the boat-house upon the calm bosom of the lovely Charles rocking softly to the little waves that lapped her sides.

The day had been oppressive, but upon the river a refreshing breeze was blowing now that the sun had gone down. For the time all Dianthe's cares left her and her tortured mind was at peace. Molly was full of life and jested and sang and laughed. She had brought her mandolin with her and gave them soft strains of delicious waltzes.

On, on they glided under the impetus of the paddle-strokes in Aubrey's skilful hands, now past the verdure-clad pine hills,

now through beds of fragrant water-lilies getting gradually farther and farther from the companionship of other pleasure-
seekers. On, into the uninhabited portion where silent woods
and long green stretches of pasture-land added a wild loneliness
to the scene.

How lovely was the evening sky with its white clouds dot-
ting the azure and the pink tinting of the sunset casting over all
its enlivening glow; how deep, and dark was the green of the
water beneath the shadowing trees. From the land came the low-
ing of cows and the sweet scent of freshly spread hay.

Suddenly Aubrey's paddle was caught and held in the
meshes of the water-lily stems that floated all about them. He
leaned far over to extricate it and in a moment the frail craft
was bottom up, its living freight struggling in the river. Once,
twice, thrice a thrilling call for help echoed over the darkening
land; then all was still.

CHAPTER X

HE expedition with which Reuel Briggs found himself
connected was made up of artists, savans and several
men—capitalists—who represented the business interests of the venture. Before the white cliffs of the English
coast were entirely lost to view, Reuel's natural propensities for
leadership were being fully recognized by the students about
him. There was an immediate demand for his professional services and he was kept busy for many days. And it was the best
panacea for a nature like his—deep and silent and self-
suppressing. He had abandoned happiness for duty; he had stifled
all those ominous voices which rose from the depth of his heart,
and said to him: "Will you ever return? and if you return will you
find your dear one? and, if you find her, will she not have
changed? will she have preserved your memory as faithfully as
you will preserve hers?

A thousand times a day while he performed his duties
mechanically, his fate haunted him—the renunciation which
called on him to give up happiness, to open to mishap the fatal
door absence. All the men of the party were more or less silent
and distrait, even Charlie Vance was subdued and thoughtful.
But Briggs suffered more than any of them, although he succeeded in affecting a certain air of indifference. As he gradually
calmed down and peace returned to his mind, he was surprised
to feel the resignation that possessed him. Some unseen presence
spoke to his inner being words of consolation and hope. He was

shown very clearly his own inability to control events, and that his fate was no longer in his own hands but ordered by a being of infinite pity and love. After hours spent in soul-communion with the spirit of Dianthe, he would sink into refreshing slumber and away in peace. Her letters were bright spots, very entertaining and describing minutely her life and daily occupation since his departure. He lived upon them during the voyage to Tripoli, sustained by the hope of finding one upon arriving at that city.

One fine evening when the sun was setting, they arrived at Tripoli. Their course lay toward the southward, and standing on deck, Reuel watched the scene—a landscape strange in form, which would have delighted him and filled him with transports of joy; now he felt something akin to indifference.

The ripples that flit the burnished surface of the long undulating billows tinkled continually on the sides of the vessel. He was aware of a low-lying spectral-pale band of shore. That portion of Africa whose nudity is only covered by the fallow mantle of the desert gave a most sad impression to the gazer. The Moors call it "Bled el Ateusch," the Country of Thirst; and, as there is an intimate relation between the character of a country and that of its people, Reuel realized vividly that the race who dwelt here must be different from those of the rest of the world.

"Ah! that is our first glimpse of Africa, is it?" said Adonis's voice, full of delight, beside him.

He turned to see his friend offering him a telescope. "At last we are here. In the morning we shall set our feet on the enchanted ground."

In the distance one could indeed make out upon the deep blue of the sky the profile of Djema el Gomgi, the great mosque on the shores of the Mediterranean. At a few cable lengths away the city smiles at them with all the fascination of a modern Cleopatra, circled with an oasis of palms studded with hundreds of domes and minarets. Against a sky of amethyst the city stands forth with a penetrating charm. It is the eternal enchantment of the cities of the Orient seen at a distance; but, alas! set foot within them, the illusion vanishes and disgust seizes you. Like beautiful bodies they have the appearance of life, but within the worm of decay and death eats ceaselessly.

At twilight in this atmosphere the city outlines itself faintly, then disappears in dusky haze. One by one the stars came into the sky until the heavens were a twinkling blaze; the sea murmured even her soft refrain and slept with the transparency of a mirror, flecked here and there with fugitive traces of phosophorescence.

The two young men stood a long time on the deck gazing toward the shore.

"Great night!" exclaimed Adonis at length with a long-drawn sigh of satisfaction. "It promises to be better than anything Barnum has ever given us even at a dollar extra reserved seat."

Reuel smiled in spite of himself; after all, Charlie was a home-line warranted to ward off homesickness. On board there was the sound of hurrying feet and a murmur of suppressed excitement, but it had subsided shortly; an hour later "sleep and oblivion reigned over all."

In the morning, amid the bustle of departure the mail came on board. There were two letters for Reuel. He seated himself in the seclusion of the cabin safe from prying eyes. Travelling across the space that separated him from America, his thoughts were under the trees in the garden of Vance Hall. In the fresh morning light he thought he could discern the dress of his beloved as she came toward him between the trees.

Again he was interrupted by Charlie's jolly countenance. He held an open letter in his hand. "There, Doc., there's

Molly's letter. Read it, read it; don't have any qualms of con-science about it. There's a good bit in it concerning the Madam, see? I thought you'd like to read it." Then he saun-tered away to talk with Jim Titus about the supplies for the trip across the desert.

Jim was proving himself a necessary part of the expedition. He was a Negro of the old régime who felt that the Anglo-Saxon was appointed by God to rule over the African. He showed his thoughts in his obsequious manner, his subservient "massa," and his daily conversation with those about him. Jim superintended the arrangement of the table of the exploring party, haggled over prices with the hucksters, quarreled with the galley cooks and ended by doing all the cooking for his party in addition to keeping his eye on "Massa Briggs." All of this was very pleasant, but sometimes Reuel caught a gleam in Jim's furtive black eye which set him thinking and wondering at the latter's great interest in himself; but he accounted for this because of Livingston's admonitions to Jim to "take care of Dr. Briggs."

Willing or not, the company of travellers were made to take part in the noisy scene on deck when a horde of dirty rascals waylaid them, and after many uses and combination of all sorts over a few cents, they and their luggage were transported to the Custom House. "Ye gods!" exclaimed Charlie in deep disgust, "what a jostling, and what a noise."

All the little world about them was in an uproar, everyone signalling, gesticulating, speaking at once. Such a fray bewilders a civilized man, but those familiar with Southern exuberance regard it tranquilly, well knowing the disorder is more apparent than real. Those of the party who were familiar with the scene, looked on highly amused at the bewilderment of the novices.

Most of them had acquired the necessary art of not hurry-ing, and under their direction the examination of the baggage proceeded rapidly. Presently, following a robust porter, they had traversed an open place filled with the benches and chairs of a "café," and soon the travellers were surprised and amused to find themselves objects of general curiosity. Coffee and nargiles were there merely as a pretext, in reality the gathering was in their honor. The names of the members of the expedition were known, together with its object of visiting Meroe of ancient fame, the arrival of such respectable visitors is a great event. Then, too, Tripoli is the natural road by which Africa has been attacked by many illustrious explorers because of the facility of communication with the country of the Blacks. Nowhere in northern Africa does the Great Desert advance so near the sea. The Atlas range rises from the Atlantic coast, extending far eastward. This range loses itself in the gulf of Little Syrta, and the vast, long-pent-up element, knowing no more barrier, spreads its yellow, sandy waves as far as the Nile, enveloping the last half-submerged summits which form a rosary of oases.

Under the Sultan's rule Tripoli has remained the capital of a truly barbaric state, virgin of improvements, with just enough dilapidated abandon, dirt and picturesqueness to make the delight of the artist. Arabs were everywhere; veiled women looked at the Christians with melting eyes above their wrappings. Mohammedanism, already twelve centuries old, has, after a period of inactivity, awakened anew in Africa, and is rapidly spreading. Very unlike the Christians, the faithful of today are the same fervid Faithful of Omar and Mohammed. Incredulity, indifference, so widely spread among other sects are unknown to them.

Supper-time found the entire party seated on the floor around a well-spread tray, set on a small box. They had taken possession of the one living-room of a mud house. It was primitive but clean. A post or two supported the thatched ceiling.

There were no windows. The furniture consisted of a few rugs and cushions. But the one idea of the party being sleep, they were soon sunk in a profound and dreamless slumber.

The next day and the next were spent in trying to gain an audience with the Sheik Mohammed Abdallah, and the days lengthened into weeks and a month finally rolled into oblivion. Meantime there were no letters for Dr. Briggs and Charlie Vance. Everyone else in the party had been blessed with many letters, even Jim was not forgotten.

Reuel had learned to be patient in the dolce far niente of the East, but not so Charlie. He fumed and fretted continually after the first weeks had passed. But promptly at two, one hot afternoon the Sheik knocked at the door of their hut. He was a handsome man of forty years—tall, straight, with clear brown eyes, good features, a well-shaped moustache and well-trimmed black beard. Authority surrounded him like an atmosphere. He greeted the party in French and Arabic and invited them to his house where a feast was spread for them. Presents were given and received and then they were introduced to Ababdis, an owner of camels who was used to leading parties into the wilderness. After much haggling over prices, it was decided to take fifteen camels and their drivers. Supplies were to consist of biscuit, rice, tea, sugar, coffee, wax candles, charcoal and a copious supply of water bags. It was decided not to start until Monday, after the coming of the mail, which was again due. After leaving Tripoli, it was doubtful when they would receive news from America again. The mail came. Again Jim was the only one who received a letter from the United States. Reuel handed it to him with a feeling of homesickness and a sinking of the heart.

Monday morning found them mounted and ready for the long journey across the desert to the first oasis. From the back of a camel Charlie Vance kept the party in good humor with his quaint remarks. "Say, Doc., it's worth the price. How I wish the pater, your wife and Molly could see us now. Livingston wouldn't do a thing to these chocolate colored gentry of Arabia."

"And Miss Scott? where does she come in?" questioned Reuel with an assumption of gaiety he was far from feeling.

"Oh," replied Charlie, not at all nonplussed. "Cora isn't in the picture; I'm thinking of a houri."

"Same old thing, Charlie—the ladies?"

"No," said Charlie, solemnly. "It's business this time. Say, Briggs, the sight of a camel always makes me a child again. The long-necked beast is inevitably associated in my mind with Barnum's circus and playing hookey. Pop wants me to put out my sign and go in for business, but the show business suits me better. For instance," he continued with a wave of his hand including the entire caravan, "Arabs, camels, stray lions, panthers, scorpions, serpents, explorers, etc., with a few remarks by yours truly, to the accompaniment of the band—always the band you know, would make an interesting show—a sort of combination of Barnum and Kiralfy. The houris would do Kiralfy's act, you know. There's money in it."

"Were you ever serious in your life, Charlie?"

"What the deuce is the need of playing funeral all the time, tell me that, Briggs, will you?"

The great desert had the sea's monotony. They rode on and on hour after hour. The elements of the view were simple. Narrow valleys and plains bounded by picturesque hills lay all about them. The nearer hills to the right had shoulders and hollows at almost regular intervals, and a sky-line of an almost regular curve. Under foot the short grass always seemed sparse, and the low sage-shrubs rather dingy, but as they looked over the plain stretching away in every direction, it had a distinctly green tint. They saw occasionally a red poppy and a purple iris.

Not a tree was to be seen, nor a rock. Sometimes the land lay absolutely level and smooth, with hardly a stone larger than a bean. The soft blue sky was cloudless, the caravan seemed to be the only living creature larger than a gazelle in the great solitude. Even Reuel was aroused to enthusiasm by the sight of a herd of these graceful creatures skimming the plain. High in the air the larks soared and sang.

As they went southward the hot sun poured its level rays upon them, and the song of the drivers was a relief to their thoughts. The singing reminded travellers of Venetian gondoliers, possessing as it did the plaintive sweetness of the most exquisite European airs. There was generally a leading voice answered by a full chorus. Reuel thought he had never heard music more fascinating. Ababdis would assume the leading part. "Ah, when shall I see my family again; the rain has fallen and made a canal between me and my home. Oh, shall I never see it more?" Then would follow the chorus of drivers: "Oh, what pleasure, what delight, to see my family again; when I see my father, mother, brothers, sisters, I will hoist a flag on the head of my camel for joy!" About the middle of the week they were making their way over the Great Desert where it becomes an elevated plateau crossed by rocky ridges, with intervening sandy plains mostly barren, but with here and there a solitary tree, and sometimes a few clumps of grass. The caravan was skirting the base of one of these ridges, which culminated in a cliff looking, in the distance, like a half-ruined castle, which the Arabs believed to be enchanted. Reuel determined to visit this cliff, and saying nothing to any one, and accompanied only by Jim and followed by the warnings of the Arabs to beware of lions, they started for the piles of masonry, which they reached in a couple of hours. The moon rose in unclouded splendor, and Moore's lines came to his heart:

"O, such a blessed night as this,
    I often think if friends were near,
  How we should feel, and gaze with bliss
    Upon the moonlight scenery here."

He strolled into the royal ruin, stumbling over broken carvings, and into hollows concealed by luminous plants, beneath whose shades dwelt noisome things that wriggled away in the marvelous white light. Climbing through what was once a door, he stepped out on a ledge of masonry, that hung sheer seven hundred feet over the plain. Reuel got out his pipe and it was soon in full blast, while the smoker set to building castles in the curls of blue smoke, that floated lightly into space. Jim with the guns waited for him at the foot of the hill.

Under the influence of the soothing narcotic and the spell of the silver moon, Reuel dreamed of fame and fortune he would carry home to lay at a little woman's feet. Presently his castle-building was interrupted by a low wail—not exactly the mew of a cat, nor yet the sound of a lute.

Again the sound.

What could it be?

"Ah, I have it!" muttered Reuel; "it's the Arabs singing in the camp."

Little did he imagine that within ten paces of him crouched an enormous leopard.

Little did he imagine that he was creeping, creeping toward him, as a cat squirms at a bird.

He sat on the ruined ledge of the parapet, within two feet of the edge; seven hundred feet below the desert sand glittered like molten silver in the gorgeous moonlight.

He was unarmed, having given Jim his revolver to hold.

Reuel sat there entirely unconscious of danger; presently a

vague feeling struck him, not of fear, not of dread, but a feeling that if he turned his head he would see an enemy, and without knowing why, he slowly turned his head.

Great heavens! what did he see? A thrill of horror passed through him as his eyes rested upon those of an enormous brute, glaring like hot coals set in blood-red circles.

Its mouth was wide open, its whiskers moving like the antennae of a lobster. It lay on its belly, its hindquarters raised, its forepaws planted in the tawny sand ready to spring.

The moon played on the spots of its body. The dark spots became silvered, and relapsed into darkness as the animal breathed, while its tail lashed about, occasionally whipping the sand with a peculiar swish.

How was he to withstand its spring?

The weight of its body would send him over the precipice like a shot.

Strange to say a grim satisfaction came to him at the thought that the brute must go down with him. Where could he hold? Could he clutch at anything? he asked himself.

He dared not remove his eyes from those of the leopard. He could not in fact. But in a sort of introverted glance he saw that nothing stood between him and space but a bare, polished wall, that shone white beneath moonbeams.

"Was there a loose stone—a stone that would crush in the skull of the blood-thirsty animal?" Not so much as a pebble to cast into the depths, for he had already searched for one to fling over, as people do when perched on imminences. He cried for help, "Jim! Jim! O-o-o-h, Jim!"

There came no reply; not the slightest sound broke the stillness as the sound of his cries died away.

Reuel was now cool—cool as a cucumber—so cool that he deliberately placed himself in position to receive the rush of the terrific brute. He felt himself moving gently back his right foot, shuffling it back until his heel came against an unevenness in the rock, which gave him a sort of purchase—something to back it.

He gathered himself together for a supreme effort, every nerve being at the highest condition of tension.

It is extraordinary all the thoughts that pass like lightning in a second of time, through the mind, while face to face with death. Volumes of ideas flashed through his brain as he stood on the stone ledge, with eternity awaiting him, knowing that this would be the end of all his hopes and fears and pleasant plans for future happiness, that he would go down to death in the embrace of the infuriated animal before him, its steel-like claws buried in his flesh, its fetid breath filling his nostrils. He thought of his darling love, and of how the light would go out of her existence with his death. He thought of Livingston, of the fellows who had gathered to bid him God speed, of the paragraphs in the papers. All these things came as harrowing pictures as he stood at bay in the liquid pearl of the silent moon.

The leopard began to move its hindquarters from side to side. A spring was at hand.

Reuel yelled then—yelled till the walls of the ruined castle echoed again—yelled as if he had 10,000 voices in his throat— yelled, as a man only yells when on his being heard depends his chance for dear life.

The beast turned its head sharply, and prepared to spring. For a second Briggs thought that a pantomime trick might give him a chance. What if he were to wait until the animal actually leaped, and then turn aside?

Carried forward by its own weight and momentum it would go over the ledge and be dashed to pieces on the rocks below.

It was worth trying. A drowning man catches at a straw. Instinctively Reuel measured his distance. He could step aside and let the brute pass, but that was all. The ledge was narrow. He was, unhappily, in very good condition. The seavoyage had fattened him, and it was just a chance that he could escape being carried over by the brute.

He accepted the chance.

Then came the fearful moment.

The leopard swayed a little backward!

Then, to his intense delight, he heard a shout of encouragement in Vance's well-known voice, "Coming, Briggs, coming!"

The next moment a hand was laid on his shoulder from a window above; it was Charlie, who trembling with anxiety had crept through the ruin, and, oh, blessed sight! handed Reuel his revolver.

Briggs made short work of the leopard; he let him have three barrels—all in the head.

Vance had become alarmed for the safety of his friend, and had gone to the ruin to meet him. When very nearly there, he had heard the first cry for help, and had urged his camel forward. Arrived at the castle he had found Jim apparently dead with sleep, coiled up on the warm sand. How he could sleep within sound of the piercing cries uttered by Briggs was long a mystery to the two friends.

CHAPTER XI

HE caravan had halted for the night. Professor Stone, the leader of the expedition, sat in Reuel's tent enjoying a pipe and a talk over the promising features of the enterprise. The nearer they approached the goal of their hopes—the ancient Ethiopian capital Meroe—the greater was the excitement among the leaders of the party. Charlie from his bed of rugs listened with ever-increasing curiosity to the conversation between the two men.

"It is undoubtedly true that from its position as the capital of Ethiopia and the enterpret of trade between the North and South, between the East and West, Meroe must have held vast treasures. African caravans poured ivory, frankincense and gold into the city. My theory is that somewhere under those pyramids we shall find invaluable records and immense treasure."

"Your theories may be true, Professor, but if so, your discoveries will establish the primal existence of the Negro as the most ancient source of all that you value in modern life, even antedating Egypt. How can the Anglo-Saxon world bear the establishment of such a theory?" There was a hidden note of sarcasm in his voice which the others did not notice.

The learned savan settled his glasses and threw back his head.

"You and I, Briggs, know that the theories of prejudice are swept away by the great tide of facts. It is a *fact* that Egypt drew from Ethiopia all the arts, sciences and knowledge of which she was mistress. The very soil of Egypt was pilfered by the Nile from the foundations of Meroe. I have even thought," he continued meditatively, "that black was the original color of man in prehistoric times. You remember that Adam was made from the earth; what more natural than that he should have retained the color of the earth? What puzzles me is not the origin of the Blacks, but of the Whites. Miriam was made a leper outside the tents for punishment; Naaman was a leper until cleansed. It is a question fraught with big possibilities which God alone can solve. But of this we are sure—all records of history, sacred and profane, unite in placing the Ethiopian as the primal race."

"Gee whiz!" exclaimed Charlie from his bed on the floor. "Count me out!"

"Don't touch upon the origin of the Negro; you will find yourself in a labyrinth, Professor. That question has provoked more discussion than any other concerning the different races of man on the globe. Speculation has exhausted itself, yet the mystery appears to remain unsolved."

"Nevertheless the Biblical facts are very explicit, and so simple as to force the very difficulties upon mankind that Divinity evidently designed to avoid."

"The relationship existing between the Negro and other people of the world is a question of absorbing interest. For my part, I shall be glad to add to my ethnological knowledge by anything we may learn at Meroe." Thus speaking Reuel seemed desirous of dismissing the subject. More conversation followed on indifferent subjects, and presently the Professor bade them good night and retired to his own tent.

Reuel employed himself in making entries in his journal, Charlie continued to smoke, at times evincing by a musical snore that he was in the land of dreams. Jim sat at some distance reading a letter that he held in his hand.

The night was sultry, the curtains of the tent undrawn; from out the silent solitude came the booming call of a lion to his mate.

Suddenly a rush of balmy air seemed to pass over the brow of the scribe, and a dim shadow fell across the tent door. It was the form of the handsome Negress who had appeared to Dianthe, and signed herself "Mira."

There was no fear in Reuel's gaze, no surprise; it was as if a familiar and welcome visitor had called upon him. For a moment an impulse to spring away into the wide, wide realms of air, seemed to possess him; the next, the still, dreamy ecstasy of a past time; and then he saw Jim—who sat directly behind him—placed like a picture on his very table. He saw him knit his brow, contract his lip, and then, with a face all seamed with discontent, draw from his vest a letter, seemingly hidden in a private pocket, reading thus:—

"Use your discretion about the final act, but be sure the letters are destroyed. I have advised the letters sent in your care as you will probably be detailed for the mail. But to avoid mishap call for the mail for both parties. Address me at Laurel Hill—Thomas Johnson."

"A. L."

Twice did the visionary scene, passing *behind* the seer, recross his entranced eyes; and twice did the shadowy finger of the shining apparition in the tent door point, letter by letter, to the pictured page of the billet, which Jim was at that very moment perusing with his natural, and Reuel Briggs with his spiritual eyes. When both had concluded the reading, Jim put up his letter. The curtains of the tent slightly waved; a low, long sigh, like the night's wind wail, passed over the cold, damp brow of the seer. A shudder, a blank. He looked out into the desert beyond.

All was still. The stars were out for him, but the vision was gone.

Thus was explained to Reuel, by mesmeric forces, the fact that his letters had been withheld.

He had not once suspected Jim of perfidy. What did it mean? he asked himself. The letter was in Livingston's handwriting! His head swam; he could not think. Over and over again he turned the problem and then, wishing that something more definite had been given him, retired, but not to sleep.

Try as he would to throw it off, the most minute act of Jim since entering his service persisted in coming before his inner vision. The night when he was attacked by the leopard and Jim's tardiness in offering help, returned with great significance. What could he do but conclude that he was the victim of a conspiracy.

"There is no doubt about it," was his last thought as he dropped into a light doze. How long he slept he could not tell, but he woke with a wild, shrill cry in his ears: "Reuel, Reuel, save me!"

Three times it was repeated, clear, distinct, and close beside his ear, a pause between the repetitions.

He roused his sleeping friend. "Charlie, Charlie! wake up and listen!"

Charlie, still half asleep, looked with blinking eyes at the candle with dazzled sight.

"Charlie, for the love of God wake up!"

At this, so full of mortal fear were his words, Adonis shook off his drowsiness and sat up in bed, wide awake and staring at him in wonder.

"What the deuce!" he began, and then stopped, gazing in surprise at the white face and trembling hands of his friend.

"Charlie," he cried, "some terrible event has befallen

Dianthe, or like a sword hangs over our heads. Listen, listen!"

Charlie did listen but heard nothing but the lion's boom which now broke the stillness.

"I hear nothing, Reuel."

"O Charlie, are you sure?"

"Nothing but the lion. But that'll be enough if he should take it into his mind to come into camp for his supper."

"I suppose you are right, for you can hear nothing, and I can hear nothing now. But, oh Charlie! it was so terrible, and I heard it so plainly; though I daresay it was only my—Oh God! there it is again! listen! listen!"

This time Charlie heard—heard clearly and unmistakably, and hearing, felt the blood in his veins turn to ice.

Shrill and clear above the lion's call rose a prolonged wail, or rather shriek, as of a human voice rising to heaven in passionate appeal for mercy, and dying away in sobbing and shuddering despair. Then came the words:

"Charlie, brother, save me!"

Adonis sprang to his feet, threw back the curtain of the tent and looked out. All was calm and silent, not even a cloud flecked the sky where the moon's light cast a steady radiance.

Long he looked and listened; but nothing could be seen or heard. But the cry still rang in his ears and clamored at his heart; while his mind said it was the effect of imagination.

Reuel's agitation had swallowed up his usual foresight. He had forgotten his ability to resort to that far-seeing faculty which he had often employed for Charlie's and Aubrey's amusement when at home.

Charlie was very calm, however, and soothed his friend's fears, and after several ineffectual attempts to concentrate his powers for the exercise of the clairvoyant sight of the hypnotic trance, was finally able to exercise the power.

In low, murmuring cadence, sitting statuesque and rigid beneath the magnetic spell, Reuel rehearsed the terrible scene which had taken place two months before in the United States in the ears of his deeply-moved friend.

"Ah, there is Molly, poor Molly; and see your father weeps, and the friends are there and they too weep, but where is my own sweet girl, Dianthe, love, wife! No, I cannot see her, I do not find the poor maimed body of my love. And Aubrey! What! Traitor, false friend! I shall return for vengeance.

"Wake me, Charlie," was his concluding sentence.

A few upward passes of his friend's hands, and the released spirit became lord of its casket once more. Consciousness returned, and with it memory. In short whispered sentences Reuel told Vance of his suspicions, of the letter he read while it lay in Jim's hand, of his deliberate intention to leave him to his fate in the leopard's claws.

The friends laid their plans,—they would go on to Meroe, and then return instantly to civilization as fast as steam could carry them, if satisfactory letters were not waiting them from America.

CHAPTER XII

LATE one afternoon two weeks later, the caravan halted at the edge of the dirty Arab town which forms the outposts to the island of Meroe.

Charlie Vance stood in the door of his tent and let his eyes wander over the landscape in curiosity. Clouds of dust swept over the sandy plains; when they disappeared the heated air began its dance again, and he was glad to re-enter the tent and stretch himself at full length in his hammock. The mail was not yet in from Cairo, consequently there were no letters; his eyes ached from straining them for a glimpse of the Ethiopian ruins across the glassy waters of the tributaries of the Nile which encircled the island.

It was not a simple thing to come all these thousand of miles to look at a pile of old ruins that promised nothing of interest to him after all. This was what he had come for—the desolation of an African desert, and the companionship of human fossils and savage beasts of prey. The loneliness made him shiver. It was a desolation that doubled desolateness, because his healthy American organization missed the march of progress attested by the sound of hammers on unfinished buildings that told of a busy future and cosy modern homeliness. Here there was no future. No railroads, no churches, no saloons, no schoolhouses to echo the voices of merry children, no promise of the life that produces within the range of his vision. Nothing but the monotony of past centuries dead and forgotten save by a few learned savans.

As he rolled over in his hammock, Charlie told himself that next to seeing the pater and Molly, he'd give ten dollars to be able to thrust his nose into twelve inches of whiskey and soda, and remain there until there was no more. Then a flicker of memory made Charlie smile as he remembered the jollities of the past few months that he had shared with Cora Scott.

"Jolly little beggar," he mentally termed her. "I wonder what sort of a fool she'd call me if she could see me now whistling around the ragged edge of this solid block of loneliness called a desert."

Then he fell asleep and dreamed he was boating on the Charles, and that Molly was a mermaid sporting in a bed of water-lilies.

Ancient writers, among them Strabo, say that the Astabora unites its stream with the Nile, and forms the island of Meroe. The most famous historical city of Ethiopia is commonly called Carthage, but Meroe was the queenly city of this ancient people. Into it poured the traffic of the world in gold, frankincense and ivory. Diodorus states the island to be three hundred and seventy-five miles long and one hundred and twenty-five miles wide. The idea was borne in upon our travelers in crossing the Great Desert that formerly wells must have been established at different stations for the convenience of man and beast. Professor Stone and Reuel had discovered traces of a highway and the remains of cisterns which must have been marvellous in skill and prodigious in formation.

All was bustle and commotion in the camp that night. Permission had been obtained to visit and explore the ruins from the Arab governor of the Province. It had cost money, but Professor Stone counted nothing as lost that would aid in the solution of his pet theories.

The leaders of the enterprise sat together late that night,

listening to the marvellous tales told by the Professor of the city's ancient splendor, and examining closely the chart which had remained hidden for years before it fell into his hands. For twenty-five years this apostle of learning had held the key to immense wealth, he believed, in his hands. For years he had tried in vain to interest the wealthy and powerful in his scheme for finding the city described in his chart, wherein he believed lay the gold mines from which had come the streams of precious metal which made the ancient Ethiopians famous.

The paper was in a large envelope sealed with a black seal formed to resemble a lotus flower. It was addressed:

> *To the student who, having counted the cost, is resolute to once more reveal to the sceptical, the ancient glory of hoary Meroe.*

Within the envelope was a faded parchment which the Professor drew forth with trembling hands. The little company drew more closely about the improvised table and its flickering candle which revealed the faded writing to be in Arabic. There was no comment, but each one listened intently to the reader, who translated very fully as he went along.

"Be it known to you, my brother, that the great and surpassing wealth mentioned in this parchment is not to be won without braving many dangers of a deadly nature. You who may read this message, then, I entreat to consider well the perils of your course. Within the mines of Meroe, four days' journey from the city toward Arabia, are to be found gold in bars and gold in flakes, and diamonds, and rubies whose beauty excels all the jewels of the earth. For some of them were hidden by the priests of Osiris that had adorned the crown of the great Semiramis, and royal line of Queen Candace, even from ancient Babylon's pillage these jewels came, a spectacle glorious beyond compare. There, too, is the black diamond of Senechus's crown (Senechus who suffered the captivity of Israel by the Assyrians), which exceeds all imagination for beauty and color.

"All these jewels with much treasure beside you will gain by following my plain directions.

"Four days' journey from Meroe toward Arabia is a city founded by men from the Upper Nile; the site is near one of its upper sources, which still has one uniform existence. This city is situated on a forked tributary, which takes its rise from a range of high, rocky mountains, almost perpendicular on their face, from which descend two streams like cataracts, about two miles apart, and form a triangle, which holds the inner city. The outer city occupies the opposite banks on either side of the streams, which after joining, form a river of considerable size, and running some five miles, loses itself in the surrounding swamps. The cities are enclosed within two great walls, running parallel with the streams. There are also two bridges with gates, connecting the inner and outer cities; two great gates also are near the mountain ranges, connecting the outer city with the agricultural lands outside the walls. The whole area is surrounded by extensive swamps, through which a passage known only to the initiated runs, and forms an impassible barrier to the ingress or egress of strangers.

"But there is another passage known to the priests and used by them, and this is the passage which the chart outlines beneath the third great pyramid, leading directly into the mines and giving access to the city.

"When Egypt rose in power and sent her hosts against the mother country, then did the priests close with skill and cunning this approach to the hidden city of refuge, where they finally retired, carrying with them the ancient records of Ethiopia's greatness, and closing forever, as they thought, the riches of her marvelous mines, to the world.

"Beneath the Sphinx' head lies the secret of the entrance, and yet not all, for the rest is graven on the sides of the cavern which will be seen when the mouth shall gape. But beware the tank to the right where dwells the sacred crocodile, still living, although centuries have rolled by and men have been gathered to the shades who once tended on his wants. And beware the fifth gallery to the right where abide the sacred serpents with jewelled crowns, for of a truth are they terrible.

"This the writer had from an aged priest whose bones lie embalmed in the third pyramid above the Sphinx."

With this extraordinary document a chart was attached, which, while an enigma to the others, seemed to be perfectly clear to Professor Stone.

The letter ended abruptly, and the chart was a hopeless puzzle to the various eyes that gazed curiously at the straggling outlines.

"What do you make of it, Professor?" asked Reuel, who with all his knowledge, was at sea with the chart. "We have been looking for mystery, and we seem to have found it."

"What do I make of it? Why, that we shall find the treasure and all return home rich," he replied the scholar testily.

"Rubbish!" snorted Charlie with fine scorn.

"How about the sacred crocodile and the serpents? My word, gentlemen, if you find the back door key of the Sphinx' head, there's a chance that a warm welcome is awaiting us."

Charlie's words met with approval from the others, but the Professor and Reuel said nothing. There was silence for a time, each man drawing at his pipe in silent meditation.

"Well, I'm only travelling for pleasure, so it matters not to me how the rest of you elect to shuffle off this mortal coil, I intend to get some fun out of this thing," continued Charlie.

There was a shout of laughter from his companions.

"Pleasure!" cried one. "O Lord! You've come to the wrong place. This is business, solid business. If we get out with our skins it will be something to be thankful for."

"Well," said Reuel, rousing himself from a fit of abstraction, "I come out to do business and I have determined to see the matter through if all is well at home. We'll prove whether there's a hidden city or not before we leave Africa."

The Professor grasped his hand in gratitude, and then silence fell upon the group. The curtains of the tent were thrown back. Bright fell the moonlight on the sandy plain, the Nile, the indistinct ruins of Meroe, hiding all imperfections by its magic fingers. It was wonderful sight to see the full moon looking down on the ruins of centuries. The weird light increased, the shadows lengthened and silence fell on the group, broken only by the low tones of Professor Stone as he told in broken sentences the story of ancient Ethiopia.

"For three thousand years the world has been mainly indebted for its advancement to the Romans, Greeks, Hebrews, Germans and Anglo-Saxons; but it was otherwise in the first years. Babylon and Egypt—Nimrod and Mizraim—both descendants of Ham—led the way, and acted as the pioneers of mankind in the untrodden fields of knowledge. The Ethiopians, therefore, manifested great superiority over all the nations among whom they dwelt, and their name became illustrious throughout Europe, Asia and Africa.

"The father of this distinguished race was Cush, the grandson of Noah, an Ethiopian.

"Old Chaldea, between the Euphrates and Tigris rivers, was the first home of the Cushites. Nimrod, Ham's grandson, founded Babylon. The Babylonians early developed the energy of mind which made their country the first abode of civilization. Canals covered the land, serving the purposes of traffic, defense and irrigation. Lakes were dug and stored with water, dykes built along the banks of rivers to fertilize the land, and it is not surprising to learn that from the earliest times Babylonia was crowded with populous cities. This grandeur was brought about by Nimrod the Ethiopian."

"Great Scott!" cried Charlie, "you don't mean to tell me that all this was done by *niggers?*"

The Professor smiled. Being English, he could not appreciate Charlie's horror at its full value.

"Undoubtedly your Afro-Americans are a branch of the wonderful and mysterious Ethiopians who had a prehistoric existence of magnificence, the full record of which is lost in obscurity.

"We associate with the name 'Chaldea' the sciences of astronomy and philosophy and chronology. It was to the Wise Men of the East to whom the birth of Christ was revealed; they were Chaldeans—of the Ethiopians. Eighty-eight years before the birth of Abraham, these people, known in history as 'Shepherd Kings,' subjugated the whole of Upper Egypt, which they held in bondage more than three hundred years."

"It is said that Egyptian civilization antedates that of Ethiopia," broke in Reuel. "How do you say, Professor?"

"Nothing of the sort, nothing of the sort. I know that in connecting Egypt with Ethiopia, one meets with most bitter denunciation from most modern scholars. Science has done its best to separate the race from Northern Africa, but the evidence is with the Ethiopians. If I mistake not, the ruins of Meroe will prove my words. Traditions with respect to Memnon connect Egypt and Ethiopia with the country at the head of the Nile. Memnon personifies the ethnic identity of the two races.

Ancient Greeks believed it. All the traditions of Armenia, where lies Mt. Ararat, are in accordance with this fact. The Armenian geography applies the name of Cush to four great regions— Media, Persia, Susiana, Asia, or the whole territory between the Indus and the Tigris. Moses of Chorene identifies Belus, king of Babylon with Nimrod.

"But the Biblical tradition is paramount to all. In it lies the greatest authority that we have for the affiliation of nations, and it is delivered to us very simply and plainly: 'The sons of Ham were Cush and Mizraim and Phut and Canaan . . . and Cush begot Nimrod . . . and the beginning of his kingdom was Babel and Erech and Accad and Calneh, in the land of Shinar.' It is the best interpretation of this passage to understand it as asserting that the four races—Egyptians, Ethiopians, Libyans and Canaanites—were ethnically connected, being all descended from Ham; and that the primitive people of Babylon were a subdivision of one of these races; namely, of the Cushite or Ethiopian.

"These conclusions have lately received important and unexpected confirmation from the results of linguistic research. After the most remarkable of Mesopotamian mounds had yielded their treasures, and supplied the historical student with numerous and copious documents, bearing upon the history of the great Assyrian and Babylonian empires, it was determined to explore Chaldea proper, where mounds of considerable height marked the site of several ancient cities. Among unexpected results was the discovery of a new form of speech, differing greatly from the later Babylonian language. In grammatical structure this ancient tongue resembles dialects of the Turanian family, but its vocabulary has been pronounced to be decidedly Cushite or Ethiopian; and the modern languages to which it approaches nearest are thought to be the Mahen of Southern Arabia and the Galla of Abyssinia. Thus comparative philology appears to confirm old traditions. An Eastern Ethiopia instead of being the invention of bewildered ignorance, is rather a reality which it will require a good deal of scepticism to doubt, and the primitive race that bore sway in Chaldea proper belongs to this ethnic type. Meroe was the queenly city of this great people."

"It is hard to believe your story. From what a height must this people have fallen to reach the abjectness of the American Negro," exclaimed a listener.

"True," replied the Professor. "But from what a depth does history show that the Anglo-Saxon has climbed to the position of the first people of the earth today."

Charlie Vance said nothing. He had suffered so many shocks from the shattering of cherished idols since entering the country of mysteries that the power of expression had left him.

"Twenty-five years ago, when I was still a young man, the camel-driver who accompanied me to Thebes sustained a fatal accident. I helped him in his distress, and to show his gratitude he gave me the paper and chart I have shown you tonight. He was a singular man, black hair and eyes, middle height, dark-skinned, face and figure almost perfect, he was proficient in the dialects of the region, besides being master of the purest and most ancient Greek and Arabic. I believe he was a native of the city he described.

"He believed that Ethiopia antedated Egypt, and helped me materially in fixing certain data which time has proved to be correct. He added a fact which the manuscript withholds,—that from lands beyond unknown seas, to which many descendants of Ethiopia had been borne as slaves, should a king of ancient line—an offspring of that Ergamenes who lived in the reign of the second Ptolemy—return and restore the former glory of the race. The preservation of this hidden city is for his reception. This Arab also declared that Cush was his progenitor."

"That's bosh. How would they know their future king after centuries of obscurity passed in strange lands, and amalgamation with other races?" remarked the former speaker.

"I asked him that question; he told me that every descendant of the royal line bore a lotus-lily in the form of a birthmark upon his breast."

It might have been the unstable shadows of the moon that threw a tremulous light upon the group, but Charlie Vance was sure that Reuel Briggs started violently at the Professor's words.

One by one the men retired to rest, each one under the spell of the mysterious forces of a past life that brooded like a mist over the sandy plain, the dark Nile rolling sluggishly along within a short distance of their camp, and the ruined city now a magnificent Necropolis. The long shadows grew longer, painting the scene into beauty and grandeur. The majesty of death surrounded the spot and its desolation spoke in trumpet tones of the splendor which the grave must cover, when even the memory of our times shall be forgotten.

CHAPTER XIII

NEXT morning the camp was early astir before the dawn; and before the sun was up, breakfast was over and the first boatload of the explorers was standing on the site of the ruins watching the unloading of the apparatus for opening solid masonry and excavating within the pyramids.

The feelings of every man in the party were ardently excited by the approach to the city once the light of the world's civilization. The great French writer, Volney, exclaimed when first his eyes beheld the sight, "How are we astonished when we reflect that to the race of Negroes, the object of our extreme contempt, we owe our arts, sciences and even the use of speech!"

From every point of view rose magnificent groups of pyramids rising above pyramids. About eighty of them remaining in a state of partial preservation. The principal one was situated on a hill two and a half miles from the river, commanding an extensive view of the plain. The explorers found by a hasty examination that most of them could be ascended although their surfaces were worn quite smooth. That the pyramids were places of sepulture they could not doubt. From every point of view the sepulchres were imposing; and they were lost in admiration and wonder with the first superficial view of the imposing scene.

One of the approaches or porticoes was most interesting, the roof being arched in regular masonic style, with what may be called a keystone. Belonging without doubt to the remotest ages, their ruined and defaced condition was attributed by the scientists to their great antiquity. The hieroglyphics which covered the monuments were greatly defaced. A knowledge of these characters in Egypt was confined to the priests, but in Ethiopia they were understood by all showing that even in that remote time and place learning and the arts had reached so high a state as to be diffused among the common people.

For a time the explorers wandered from ruin to ruin, demoralized as to routine work, gazing in open astonishment at the wonders before them. Many had visited Thebes and Memphis and the Egyptian monuments, but none had hoped to find in this neglected corner, so much of wonder and grandeur. Within the pyramids that had been opened to the curious eye, they found the walls covered with the pictures of scenes from what must have been the daily life,—death, burial, marriage, birth, triumphal processions, including the spoils of war.

Reuel noticed particularly the figure of a queen attired in long robe, tight at neck and ankles, with closely fitted legs. The Professor called their attention to the fact that the entire figure was dissimilar to those represented in Egyptian sculpture. The figure was strongly marked by corpulency, a mark of beauty in Eastern women. This rotundity is the distinguishing feature of Ethiopian sculpture, more bulky and clumsy than Egypt, but pleasing to the eye.

The queen held in one hand the lash of Osiris, and in the other a lotus flower. She was seated on a lion, wearing sandals resembling those specimens seen in Theban figures. Other figures grouped about poured libations to the queen, or carried the standards graced and ornamented by the figures of the jackal, ibis and hawk. At the extremity of each portico was the representation of a monolithic temple, above which were the traces of a funeral boat filled with figures.

Professor Stone told them that Diodorus mentions that

some of the Ethiopians preserved the bodies of their relatives in glass cases (probably alabaster), in order to have them always before their eyes. These porticoes, he thought, might have been used for that purpose. The hair of the women was dressed in curls above the forehead and in ringlets hanging on their shoulders.

One who had visited the chief galleries of Europe holding the treasures accumulated from every land, could not be unmoved at finding himself on the site of the very metropolis where science and art had their origin. If he had admired the architecture of Rome and the magnificent use they had made of the arch in their baths, palaces and temples, he would be, naturally, doubly interested at finding in desolate Meroe the origin of that discovery. The beautiful sepulchres of Meroe would give to him evidence of the correctness of the historical records. And then it was borne in upon him that where the taste for the arts had reached such perfection, one might rest assured that other intellectual pursuits were not neglected nor the sciences unknown. Now, however, her schools are closed forever; not a vestige remaining. Of the houses of her philosophers, not a stone rests upon another; and where civilization and learning once reigned, ignorance and barbarism have reassumed their sway.

This is the people whose posterity has been denied a rank among the human race, and has been degraded into a species of talking baboons!

> *"Land of the mighty Dead!*
> *There science once display'd*
> *And art, their charms;*
> *There awful Pharaohs swayed*
>
> *Great nations who obeyed;*
> *There distant monarchs laid*

Their vanquished arms.
"They hold us in survey—

They cheer us on our way—
They loud proclaim
From pyramidal hall—
From Carnac's sculptured wall—
From Thebes they loudly call—
'Retake your fame!'

"Arise and now prevail
O'er all your foes;
In truth and righteousness—
In all the arts of peace—
Advance and still increase,
Though hosts oppose."

Under the inspiration of the moment, Charlie, the irrepressible, mounted to the top of the first pyramid, and from its peak proceeded to harangue his companions, lugging in the famous Napoleon's: "From the heights of yonder Pyramids forty centuries are contemplating you," etc. This was admirably done, and the glances and grimaces of the eloquent young American must have outvied in ugliness the once gracious-countenanced Egyptian Sphinx.

We may say here that before the excavations of the explorers were ended, they found in two of the pyramids, concealed treasures,—golden plates and tables that must have been used by the priests in their worship. Before one enormous image was a golden table, also of enormous proportions. The seats and steps were also of gold, confirming the ancient Chaldean records which tells of 800 talents of metal used in constructing this statue.

There was also a statue of Candace, seated in a golden chariot. On her knees crouched two enormous silver serpents, each weighing thirty talents. Another queen (Professor Stone said it must be Dido from certain peculiar figures) carried in her right hand a serpent by the head, in her left hand a sceptre garnished with precious stones.

All of this treasure was collected finally, after indemnifying the government, and carefully exported to England, where it rests today in the care of the Society of Geographical Research.

They never forgot that sunset over the ancient capital of Ethiopia at the close of the first day spent on the city's site, in the Desert. The awe-inspiring Pyramids throwing shadows that reminded one of the geometrical problems of his student days; the backsheesh-loving Arabs, in the most picturesque habiliments and attitudes; the patient camels, the tawny sands, and the burnished coppery sunlight! They had brought tents with them, leaving the most of the outfit on the opposite bank under the care of Jim Titus, whom Reuel had desired the professor to detail for that duty. Somehow since his adventure in the ruins with the leopard, and the mysterious letter-reading, he had felt a deep-seated mistrust of the docile servant. He concluded not to keep him any nearer his person than circumstances demanded. In this resolve Charlie Vance concurred; the two friends resolved to keep an eye on Titus, and Ababdis was sent for the mail.

Reuel Briggs had changed much. Harassed by anxieties which arose from his wife's silence, at the end of two months he was fast becoming a misanthrope. Charlie felt anxious as he looked at him walking restlessly up and down in the pale moonlight, with fiery eyes fixed on space. Charlie suppressed his own feelings over the silence of his father and sister to comfort Reuel.

"You ought not, my dear Briggs," he would say. "Come, for

heaven's sake shake off that sadness which may make an end of you before you are aware." Then he would add, jestingly, "Decidedly, you regret the leopard's claws!"

On this night the excitement of new scenes had distracted the thoughts of both men from their homes, and they lay smoking in their hammocks before the parted curtains of the tent lazily watching Ababdis advancing with a bundle in his hand. It was the long expected mail!

CHAPTER XIV

T was some three weeks after this before Briggs was able to assume his duties. The sudden shock of the news of his wife's death over-weighted a brain already strained to the utmost. More than once they despaired of his life—Professor Stone and Vance, who had put aside his own grief to care for his friend. Slowly the strong man had returned to life once more. He did not rave or protest; Fate had no power to move him more; the point of anguish was passed, and in its place succeeded a dumb stupidity more terrible by far, though far more blessed.

His love was dead. He himself was dead for any sensibility of suffering that he possessed. So for many days longer he lay in his hammock seemingly without a thought of responsibility.

They had carried him back to the camp across the river, and there he spent the long days of convalescence. What did he think of all day as he moved like a shadow among the men or swung listlessly in the hammock? Many of the men asked themselves that question as they gazed at Briggs. One thought repeated itself over and over in his brain, "Many waters cannot quench love, neither can the floods drown it." "Many waters"—"many waters"—the words whispered and sung appealingly, invitingly, in his ears all day and all night. "Many waters, many waters."

One day he heard them tell of the removal of the door in the pyramid two and one-half miles on the hill. They had found the Sphinx' head as described in the manuscript, but had been unable to move it with any instrument in their possession. Much to his regret, Professor Stone felt obliged to give the matter up and content himself with the valuable relics he had found. The gold mines, if such there were, were successfully hidden from searchers, and would remain a mystery.

The white orb of the moon was high in the heavens; the echoless sand gave back no sound; that night Reuel rose, took his revolver and ammunition, and leaving a note for Vance telling him he had gone to the third pyramid and not to worry, he rowed himself over to Meroe. He had no purpose, no sensation. Once he halted and tried to think. His love was dead:—that was the one fact that filled his thoughts at first. Then another took its place. Why should he live? Of course not; better rejoin her where parting was no more. He would lose himself in the pyramid. The manuscript had spoken of dangers—he would seek them.

As he went on the moon rose in full splendor behind him. Some beast of the night plunged through a thicket along the path.

The road ascended steadily for a mile or more, crossing what must have once been carriage drives. Under the light of the setting moon the gradually increasing fertility of the ground shone silver-white. Arrived at the top of the hill, he paused to rest and wipe the perspiration from his face. After a few minutes' halt, he plunged on and soon stood before the entrance of the gloomy chamber; as he stumbled along he heard a low, distinct hiss almost beneath his feet. Reuel jumped and stood still. He who had been desirous of death but an hour before obeyed the first law of nature. Who can wonder? It was but the re-awakening of life within him, and that care for what has been entrusted to us by Omnipotence, will remain until death has numbed our senses.

The dawn wind blew all about him. He would do no more until the dawn. Presently the loom of the night lifted and he could see the outlines of the building a few yards away. From his position he commanded the plain at his feet as level as a sea. The shadows grew more distinct, then without warning, the red dawn shot up behind him. The sepulchre before him flushed the color of blood, and the light revealed the horror of its emptiness.

Fragments of marble lay about him. It seemed to the lonely watcher that he could hear the sound of the centuries marching by in the moaning wind and purposeless dust.

The silence and sadness lay on him like a pall and seemed to answer to the desolation of his own life.

For a while he rambled aimlessly from wall to wall examining the gigantic resting place of the dead with scrupulous care. Here were ranged great numbers of the dead in glass cases; up and up they mounted to the vaulted ceiling. His taper flickered in the sombreness, giving but a feeble light. The air grew cold and damp as he went on. Once upon a time there had been steps cut in the granite and leading down to a well-like depression near the center of the great chamber. Down he went holding the candle high above his head as he carefully watched for the Sphinx' head. He reached a ledge which ran about what was evidently once a tank. The ledge ran only on one side. He looked about for the Sphinx; unless it was here he must retrace his steps, for the ledge ran only a little way about one side of the chamber.

He was cold and damp, and turned suddenly to retrace his steps, when just in front of him to the left the candle's light fell full on the devilish countenance of the Ethiopian Sphinx.

He moved quickly toward it; and then began an examination of the figure. As he stepped backward his foot crushed through a skull; he retreated with a shudder. He saw now that he stood in a space of unknown dimensions. He fancied he saw rows of pillars flickering drunkenly in the gloom. The American man is familiar with many things because of the range of his experience, and Reuel Briggs was devoid of fear, but in that moment he tasted the agony of pure, physical terror. For the first time since he received his letters from home, he was himself again filled with pure, human nature. He turned to retrace his steps; something came out of the darkness like a hand, passed before his face emitting a subtle odor as it moved; he sank upon the ground and consciousness left him.

*   *   *   *   *

From profound unconsciousness, deep, merciful, oblivious to pain and the flight of time, from the gulf of the mysterious shadows wherein earth and heaven are alike forgotten, Reuel awoke at the close of the fourth day after his entrance into the Great Pyramid. That Lethean calm induced by narcotic odors, saved his reason. Great pain, whether physical or mental, cannot last long, and human anguish must find relief or take it.

A soft murmur of voices was in his ears as he languidly unclosed his eyes and gazed into the faces of a number of men grouped about the couch on which he lay, who surveyed him with looks of respectful admiration and curiosity mingled with awe. One of the group appeared to be in authority, for the others listened to him with profound respect as they conversed in low tones, and were careful not to obtrude their opinions.

Gradually his senses returned to him, and Reuel could distinguish his surroundings. He gazed about him in amazement. Gone were all evidences of ruin and decay, and in their place was bewildering beauty that filled him with dazzling awe. He reclined on a couch composed of silken cushions, in a room of vast dimensions, formed of fluted columns of pure white marble upholding a domed ceiling where the light poured in through rose-colored glass in soft prismatic shades which gave a touch of fairyland to the scene.

The men beside him were strangers, and more unreal than the vast chamber. Dark-visaged, he noticed that they ranged in complexion from a creamy tint to purest ebony; the long hair which fell upon their shoulders, varied in texture from soft, waving curls to the crispness of the most pronounced African type. But the faces into which he gazed were perfect in the cut and outline of every feature; the forms hidden by soft white drapery, Grecian in effect, were athletic and beautifully moulded. Sandals covered their feet.

The eyes of the leader followed Reuel's every movement.

"Where am I?" cried Briggs impetuously, after a hurried survey of the situation.

Immediately the leader spoke to his companions in a rich voice, commanding, but with all the benevolence of a father.

"Leave us," he said. "I would be alone with the stranger."

He spoke in ancient Arabic known only to the most profound students of philology. Instantly the room was cleared, each figure vanished behind the silken curtains hanging between the columns at one side of the room.

"How came I here?" cried Reuel again.

"Peace," replied the leader, extending his arms as if in benediction above the young man's head. "You have nothing to fear. You have been brought hither for a certain purpose which will shortly be made clear to you; you shall return to your friends if you desire so to do, after the council has investigated your case. But why, my son, did you wander at night about the dangerous passages of the pyramid? Are you, too, one of those who seek for hidden treasure?"

In years the speaker was still young, not being over forty despite his patriarchal bearing. The white robe was infinitely becoming, emphasizing breadth of shoulder and chest above the silver-clasped arm's-eye like nothing he had seen save in the sculptured figures of the ruined cities lately explored. But the most striking thing about the man was his kingly countenance, combining force, sweetness and dignity in every feature. The grace of a perfect life invested him like a royal robe. The musical language flowed from his lips in sonorous accents that charmed the scholar in his listener, who, to his own great surprise and delight, found that conversation between them could be carried on with ease. Reuel could not repress a smile as he thought of the astonishment of Professor Stone if he could hear them rolling out the ancient Arabic tongue as a common carrier of thought. It seemed sacrilegious.

"But where am I?" he persisted, determined to locate his whereabouts.

"You are in the hidden city Telassar. In my people you will behold the direct descendants of the inhabitants of Meroe. We are but a remnant, and here we wait behind the protection of our mountains and swamps, secure from the intrusion of a world that has forgotten, for the coming of our king who shall restore to the Ethiopian race its ancient glory. I am Ai, his faithful prime minister."

Hopelessly perplexed by the words of the speaker, Reuel tried to convince himself that he was laboring under a wild hallucination; but his senses all gave evidence of the reality of his situation. Somewhere in Milton he had read lines that now came faintly across his memory:

> "Eden stretched her lines
> From Auran eastward to the royal tow'rs
> Of great Seleucia, built by Grecian kings,
> Or where the sons of Eden long before
> Dwelt in Telassar.

Something of his perplexity Ai must have read in his eyes, for he smiled as he said, "Not Telassar of Eden, but so like to Eden's beauties did our ancestors find the city that thus did they call it."

"Can it be that you are an Ethiopian of those early days, now lost in obscurity? Is it possible that a remnant of that once magnificent race yet dwells upon old mother Earth? You talk of having lived at Meroe; surely, you cannot mean it. Were it true, what you have just uttered, the modern world would stand aghast."

Ai bowed his head gravely. "It is even so, incredible though it may seem to you, stranger. Destroyed and abased because of her idolatries, Ethiopia's arrogance and pride have been humbled in the dust. Utter destruction has come upon Meroe the glorious, as was predicted. But there was a hope held out to the faithful worshippers of the true God that Ethiopia should stretch forth her hand unto Eternal Goodness, and that then her glory should again dazzle the world. I am of the priestly caste, and the office I hold descends from father to son, and has so done for more than six thousand years before the birth of Christ. But enough of this now; when you are fully rested and recovered from the effect of the narcotics we were forced to give you, I will talk with you, and I will also show you the wonders of our hidden city. Come with me."

Without more speech he lifted one of the curtains at the side of the room, revealing another apartment where running water in marble basins invited one to the refreshing bath. Attendants stood waiting, tall, handsome, dark-visaged, kindly, and into their hands he resigned Reuel.

Used as he was to the improvements and luxuries of life in the modern Athens, he could but acknowledge them as poor beside the combination of Oriental and ancient luxury that he now enjoyed. Was ever man more gorgeously housed than this? Overhead was the tinted glass through which the daylight fell in softened glow. In the air was the perfume and lustre of precious incense, the flash of azure and gold, the mingling of deep and delicate hues, the gorgeousness of waving plants in blossom and tall trees—palms, dates, orange, mingled with the gleaming statues that shone forth in brilliant contrast to the dark green foliage. The floor was paved with varied mosaic and dotted here and there with the skins of wild animals.

After the bath came a repast of fruit, game and wine, served him on curious golden dishes that resembled the specimens taken from ruined Pompeii. By the time he had eaten night had fallen, and he laid himself down on the silken cushions of his couch, with a feeling of delicious languor and a desire for repose. His nerves were in a quiver of excitement and he doubted his ability to sleep, but in a few moments, even while he doubted, he fell into a deep sleep of utter exhaustion.

CHAPTER XV

HEN he arose in the morning he found that his own clothing had been replaced by silken garments fashioned as were Ai's with the addition of golden clasps and belts. In place of his revolver was a jeweled dagger literally encrusted with gems.

After the bath and breakfast, Ai entered the room with his noiseless tread, and when the greetings had been said, invited him to go with him to visit the public buildings and works of Telassar. With a swift, phantom like movement, Ai escorted his guest to the farther end of the great hall. Throwing aside a curtain of rich topaz silk which draped the large entrance doors he ushered him into another apartment opening out on a terrace with a garden at its foot—a garden where a marvellous profusion of flowers and foliage ran riot amid sparkling fountains and gleaming statuary.

Through a broad alley, lined with majestic palms, they passed to the extreme end of the terrace, and turning faced the building from which they had just issued. A smile quivered for a moment on Ai's face as he noted Reuel's ill-concealed amazement. He stood for a moment stock-still, overcome with astonishment at the size and splendor of the palace that had sheltered him over night. The building was dome-shaped and of white marble, surrounded by fluted columns, and fronted by courts where fountains dashed their spray up to the blue sky, and flowers blushed in myriad colors and birds in gorgeous plumage flitted from bough to bough.

117

It appeared to Reuel that they were on the highest point of what might be best described as a horse-shoe curve whose rounded end rested on the side of a gigantic mountain. At their feet stretched a city beautiful, built with an outer and inner wall. They were in the outer city. Two streams descended like cataracts to the plain below, at some distance from each other, forming a triangle which held another city. Far in the distance like a silver thread, he could dimly discern where the rivers joined, losing themselves in union. As he gazed he recalled the description of the treasure city that Professor Stone had read to the explorers.

As far as the eye could reach stretched fertile fields; vine-yards climbed the mountain side. Again Reuel quoted Milton in his thoughts, for here was the very embodiment of his words:

"Flowers of all hue, and without thorn the rose,
Another side, umbrageous grots and caves
Of cool recess, o'er which the mantling vine
Lays forth her purple grape, and gently creeps
Luxuriant; meanwhile murmuring waters fall
Down the slope hills, dispersed, or in a lake,
That to the fringed bank with myrtle crown'd
Her crystal mirror holds, unite their streams.
The birds their choir apply; airs, vernal airs,
Breathing the smell of field and grove, attune
The trembling leaves, while universal Pan,
Knit with the Graces and the Hours in dance,
Led on th' eternal spring."

Far below he could dimly discern moving crowds; great buildings reared their stately heads towards a sky so blue and bewildering beneath the sun's bright rays that the gazer was rendered speechless with amazement. Shadowy images of past scenes and happenings flitted across his brain like transient reflection of a past perfectly familiar to him.

"Do you find the prospect fair?" asked Ai at length, breaking the settled silence.

"Fairer than I can find words to express; and yet I am surprised to find that it all seems familiar to me, as if somewhere in the past I had known just such a city as this." Ai smiled a smile of singular sweetness and content; Reuel could have sworn that there was a degree of satisfaction in his pleasure.

"Come, we will go down into the city. You who know the wonders of modern life at its zenith, tell me what lesson you learn from the wonders of a civilization which had its zenith six thousand years before Christ's birth."

"Six thousand years before Christ!" murmured Reuel in black stupidity.

"Aye: here in Telassar are preserved specimens of the highest attainments the world knew in ancient days. They tell me that in many things your modern world is yet in its infancy."

"How!" cried Reuel, "do you then hold communion with the world outside your city?"

"Certain members of our Council are permitted to visit outside the gates. Do you not remember Ababdis?"

"Our camel-driver?"

Ai bowed. "He is the member who brought us news of your arrival, and the intention of the expedition to find our city for the sake of its treasure."

More and more mystified by the words and manner of his guide, Reuel made no reply. Presently they entered a waiting palanquin and were borne swiftly toward the city. The silken curtains were drawn one side, and he could drink in the curious sights. They soon left the country behind them and entered a splendid square, where stately homes were outlined against the dense blue of the sky. A statue of an immense sphinx crouched in the center of the square, its giant head reaching far into the ethereal blue. Fountains played on either side, dashing their silvery spray beyond the extreme height of the head. Under umbrageous trees were resting-places, and on the sphinx was engraved the words: "That which hath been, is now; and that which is to be, hath already been; and God requireth that which is past."

Suddenly a crowd of men surged into the square, and a deep-toned bell sounded from a distance. Swiftly sped the bearers, urged forward by the general rush. The booming of the bell continued. They reached the end of the avenue and entered a side street, through a court composed of statues. They paused before a stately pile, towering in magnificence high in the heavens, a pile of marvellously delicate architecture worked in stone. The entrance was of incomparable magnificence. Reuel judged that the four colossal statues before it represented Rameses the Great. They were each sculptured of a single block of Syene granite of mingled red and black. They were seated on cubical stones. The four Colosses sitting there before that glittering pile produced a most imposing effect.

The steps of the temple were strewn with flowers; the doors stood open, and the music from stringed instruments vibrated upon the air. The bearers stopped at a side entrance, and at a sign from Ai, Reuel followed him into the edifice.

All was silence, save for the distant hum of voices, and the faint sound of music. They halted before a curtain which parted silently for their entrance. It was a small room, but filled with a light of soft colors; when Reuel could command his gaze, he beheld about twenty men prostrated before him. Presently they arose and each filed past him, reverently touching the hem of his white robe. Among them was Ababdis, so transformed by his gorgeous robes of office as to be almost unrecognizable.

Ai now assumed an azure robe embroidered in silver stars and crescents that formed a sunburst in shape of a Grecian cross. He then advanced towards Reuel bearing on a silken cushion a magnificent crown, where the principal aigrette was shaped as a cross set with gems priceless in value. Astounded at the sight, the young man stood motionless while it was adjusted by golden chains about his head. The gems blazed with the red of the ruby, the green of the emerald, the blue of the sapphire, the yellow of the topaz, the cold white of priceless diamonds. But dulling all the glories of precious stones, peerless in their own class, lay the center ornament—the black diamond of Senechus's crown, spoken of in Professor Stone's record. A white robe of silken stuff was added to his costume, and again his companions filed past him in deepest reverence. Reuel was puzzled to understand why so great homage was paid to him. While he turned the thought in his mind, a bugle sounded somewhere in the distance, sweet and high. Instantly, he felt a gliding motion as if the solid earth were slipping from beneath his feet, the curtains before him parted silently, and he found himself alone on a raised platform in the center of a vast auditorium, crowded with humanity. Lights twinkled everywhere; there was the fragrance of flowers, there were columns of marble draped in amber, azure and green, and glittering lamps encrusted with gems and swung by golden chains from the sides of the building. A blazing arch formed of brilliant lamps raised like a gigantic bow in the heavens and having in its center the words

"HAIL! ERGAMENES!"

in letters of sparkling fire, met his startled gaze. Then came a ringing shout from the throats of the assembled multitude,

"Ergamenes! Ergamenes!" Again and again the throng lifted up the joyous cry. Presently as Reuel stood there undecided what to do—not knowing what was expected of him, as silently as he had come, he felt the motion of the platform where he stood. The crowd faded from sight, the curtains fell; once more he stood within the little room, surrounded by his companions.

"Ababdis, Ai," he demanded, sternly, "What is the meaning of this strange happening, more like a scene from the Arabian Nights? Who is Ergamenes?"

"Thou art Ergamenes—the long-looked-for king of Ethiopia, for whose reception this city was built! But we will return to the palace, now that the people have satisfied somewhat their curiosity. At supper you shall know more."

Once more the bearers carried them swiftly beyond the confines of the city, and soon the palace walls rose before them. Reuel had hardly collected his scattered wits before he found himself seated at table and on either side of the board the Council reclined on silken cushions. His own seat was raised and placed at the head of the table. There was no talking done while what seemed to be a solemn feast was in progress. Servants passed noiselessly to and fro attending to their wants, while from an alcove the music of stringed instruments and sweetest vocal numbers was borne to their ears.

After supper, they still reclined on the couches. Then from the hidden recesses the musicians came forth, and kneeling before Reuel, one began a song in blank verse, telling the story of Ergamenes and his kingdom.

> "Hail! oh, hail Ergamenes!
> The dimmest sea-cave below thee,
> The farthest sky-arch above,
> In their innermost stillness know thee,

> *And heave with the birth of Love.*
> *"All hail!*
> *We are thine, all thine, forevermore;*
> *Not a leaf on the laughing shore,*
> *Not a wave on the heaving sea,*
> *Nor a single sigh*
> *In the boundless sky,*
> *But is vowed evermore to thee!"*

"Son of a fallen dynasty, outcast of a sunken people, upon your breast is a lotus lily, God's mark to prove your race and descent. You, Ergamenes, shall begin the restoration of Ethiopia. Blessed be the name of God for ever and ever, for wisdom and might are His, and He changeth the times and seasons; He removeth kings and countries, and setteth them up again; He giveth wisdom unto the wise, and knowledge to them that know understanding! He revealeth the deep and secret things; He knoweth what is in the darkness, and the light dwelleth with Him!

"Great were the sins of our fathers, and the white stranger was to Ethiopia but a scourge in the hands of an offended God. The beautiful temples of Babylon, filled with vessels of silver and gold, swelled the treasures of the false god Bel. Babylon, where our monarchs dwelt in splendor, once the grandest city to be found in the world. Sixty miles round were its walls, of prodigious height, and so broad that seven chariots could be driven abreast on the summit! One hundred gates of solid brass gave entrance into the city, guarded by lofty towers. Beautiful buildings rose within, richly adorned and surrounded by gardens. One magnificent royal palace was girdled by three walls, the outermost of which was seven miles and a half in compass. In its grounds rose the far-famed hanging gardens, terraces built one above one another to the height of three hundred and fifty feet, each terrace covered with thick mould, and planted with flowers and shrubs, so that the skill of man created a verdant hill on a plain. Nearly in the centre rose the lofty temple of Belus, the tower of Babel, whose builders had hoped to make its summit touch the very skies. Millions of dollars in gold were gathered in the chambers of the temple. The wealth, power and glory of the world were centered in the mighty city of Babylon.

"On the throne of this powerful city sat your forefathers, O Ergamenes!"

Part of the story had been given in recitative, one rich voice carrying grandly the monotonous notes to the accompaniment of the cornet, flute, sackbut, dulcimer and harp. Reuel had listened to the finest trained voices attempting the recitative in boasted musical circles, but never in so stately and impressive a manner as was now his privilege to hear. They continued the story.

"And Meroe, the greatest city of them all, pure-blooded Ethiopian. Once the light of the world's civilization, now a magnificent Necropolis.

"Standing at the edge of the Desert, fertile in soil, rich in the luxuries of foreign shores; into her lap caravans poured their treasures gathered from the North, South, East and West. All Africa poured into this queenly city ivory, frankincense and gold. Her colossal monuments were old before Egypt was; her wise men monopolized the learning of the ages, and in the persons of the Chaldeans have figured conspicuously the wisdom of ages since Meroe has fallen.

"Mother of ancient warfare, her horsemen and chariots were the wonder and terror of her age; from the bows of her warriors, the arrows sped like a flight of birds, carrying destruction to her foes,—a lamb in peace, a lion in time of war."

Once more the measure changed, and another voice took up the story in verse.

> *"Who will assume the bays*
> > *That the hero wore?*
> *Wreaths on the Tomb of Days*
> > *Gone evermore!*
> *Who shall disturb the brave*
> *Or one leaf of their holy grave?*
> *The laurel is vow'd to them,*
> *Leave the bay on its sacred stem!*
> *But hope, the rose, the unfading rose,*
> *Alike for slave and freeman grows!*
>
> *"On the summit, worn and hoary,*
> *Of Lybia's solemn hills,*
> *The tramp of the brave is still!*
> *And still is the poisoned dart,*
> *In the pulse of the mighty hearts,*
> *Whose very blood was glory!*
>
> *Who will assume the bays*
> > *That the hero wore?*
> *Wreaths on the Tomb of Days*
> > *Gone evermore!"*

Upon Reuel a strange force seemed to be working. If what he heard were true, how great a destiny was his! He had carefully hidden his Ethiopian extraction from the knowledge of the world. It was a tradition among those who had known him in childhood that he was descended from a race of African kings. He remembered his mother well. From her he had inherited his mysticism and his occult powers. The nature of the mystic within him was, then, but a dreamlike devotion to the spirit that had swayed his ancestors; it was the shadow of Ethiopia's power. The lotus upon his breast he knew to be a birthmark. Many a night he had been aroused from childhood's slumbers, to find his mother bending above him, candle in hand, muttering broken sentences of prayer to Almighty God as she examined his bosom by the candle's rays. He had wondered much; now he guessed the rest. Once more the clanging strings of the instruments chained his attention. The recitative was resumed.

"The Most High ruleth in the kingdom of men, and giveth it to whomsoever He will. He delivereth and rescueth, and He worketh signs and wonders in heaven and in earth. Pre-eminent in peace, invincible in war—once the masters of mankind, how have we fallen from our high estate!

"Stiff-necked, haughty, no conscience but that of intellect, awed not by God's laws, worshipping Mammon, sensual, unbelieving, God has punished us as he promised in the beginning. Gone are our ancient glories, our humbled pride cries aloud to God in the travail of our soul. Our sphinx, with passionless features, portrays the dumb suffering of our souls.

> *Their look with the reach of past ages, was wise,*
> *And the soul of eternity thought in their eyes.*

"By divine revelation David beheld the present time, when, after Christ's travail for the sins of humanity, the time of Ethiopia's atonement being past, purged of idolatry, accepting the One Only God through His Son Jesus, suddenly should come a new birth to the descendants of Ham, and Ethiopia should return to her ancient glory! Ergamenes, all hail!

"*You come from afar*
    From the land of the stranger,
The dreadful in war,
    The daring in danger;
Before him our plain
    Like Eden is lying;
Behind him remain
    But the wasted and dying.

"*The weak finds not truth,*
    Nor the patriot glory;
No hope for the youth,
    And no rest for the hoary;
O'er Ethiop's lost plains
    The victor's sword flashes,
Her sons are in chains,
    And her temples in ashes!

"*Who will assume the bays*
    That the hero wore?
Wreaths on the Tomb of Days
    Gone evermore!"

Upon his companions the song of the past of Ethiopia had a strange effect. Soothing at times, at times exciting, with the last notes from the instruments the company sprang to their feet; with flashing dark eyes, faces reflecting inward passions, they drew their short, sabrelike arms and circled about Reuel's throne with the shout "Ergamenes! Ergamenes!"

CHAPTER XVI

NCE more Reuel found himself alone with Ai. It was far into the night, but he felt sleepless and restless. At last Ai broke a long silence:

"Tell me of the country from which you come, Ergamenes. Is it true that the Ethiopian there is counted less than other mortals?"

"It is true, Ai," replied Reuel. "There, the dark hue of your skin, your waving hair with its trace of crispness, would degrade you below the estate of any man of fair hue and straight locks, belonging to any race outside the Ethiopian, for it is a deep disgrace to have within the veins even one drop of the blood you seem so proud of possessing."

"That explains your isolation from our race, then?"

Reuel bowed his head in assent, while over his face passed a flush of shame. He felt keenly now the fact that he had played the coward's part in hiding his origin. What though obstacles were many, some way would have been shown him to surmount the difficulties of caste prejudice.

"And yet, from Ethiopia came all the arts and cunning inventions that make your modern glory. At our feet the mightiest nations have worshipped, paying homage to our kings, and all nations have sought the honor of alliance with our royal families because of our strength, grandeur, riches and wisdom. Tell me of all the degradation that has befallen the unfortunate sons of Ham."

Then in the deep, mysterious silence of the night, Reuel gave in minutest detail the story of the Negro, reciting with dramatic effect the history of the wrongs endured by the modern Ethiopian.

To his queries as to the history of these mountain-dwelling Ethiopians, Ai gave the following reply:

"We are a singular people, governed by a female monarch, all having the same name, Candace, and a Council of twenty-five Sages, who are educated for periodical visits to the outer world. Queen Candace is a virgin queen who waits the coming of Ergamenes to inaugurate a dynasty of kings. Our virgins live within the inner city, and from among them Candace chooses her successor at intervals of fifteen years.

"To become a Sage, a man must be married and have at least two children; a knowledge of two out-world languages, and to pass a severe examination by the court as to education, fitness and ability. After an arduous preparation they are initiated into the secrets of this kingdom. They are chosen for life. The inner city is the virgins' court, and it is adorned with beautiful gardens, baths, schools and hospitals. When a woman marries she leaves this city for the outer one.

"We have a great temple, the one you entered, dedicated to the Supreme or Trinity. It is a masterpiece of beauty and art. The population assembles there twice a year for especial service. It seats about 12,000 persons. The Sages have seen nothing equal to it in the outer world.

Octagonal in shape, with four wings or galleries, on opposite sides; the intervening spaces are filled with great prism columns, twenty-five feet high, made of a substance like glass, malleable, elastic and pure. The effect is gorgeous. The decorations of the hall are prepared natural flowers; that is, floral garlands are subjected to the fumes of the crystal material covering them like a film and preserving their natural appearance. This is a process handed down from the earliest days of Ethiopian greatness. I am told that the modern world has not yet solved this simple process," he said with a gentle smile of ridicule.

"We preserve the bodies of our most beautiful women in this way. We suspend reflecting plates of the crystal material arranged in circles, pendant from the ceiling of the central hall, and thus the music of the instruments is repeated many times in sweetest harmony.

"We have serves at noon every seventh day, chiefly choral, in praise of the attributes of the Supreme. Our religion is a belief in One Supreme Being, the center of action in all nature. He distributed a portion of Himself at an early age to the care of man who has attained the highest development of any of His terrestrial creatures. We call this ever-living faculty or soul Ego.

"After its transition Ego has the power of expressing itself to other bodies, with like gift and form, its innate feeling; and by law of affinity, is ever striving to regain its original position near the great Unity; but the physical attractions of this beautiful world have such a fascination on the organism of man that there is ever a contention against the greater object being attained; and unless the Ego can wean the body from gross desires and raise it to the highest condition of human existence, it cannot be united to its Creator. The Ego preserves its individuality after the dissolution of the body. We believe in re-incarnation by natural laws regulating material on earth. The Ego can never be destroyed. For instance, when the body of a good man or woman dies, and the Ego is not sufficiently fitted for the higher condition of another world, it is re-associated with another body to complete the necessary fitness for heaven."

"What of the Son of man? Do you not know the necessity of belief in the Holy Trinity? Have not your Sages brought you the need of belief in God's Son?" Ai looked somewhat puzzled.

"We have heard of such a God, but have not paid much attention to it. How believe you, Ergamenes?"

"In Jesus Christ, the Son of God," replied Reuel solemnly.

"O Ergamenes, your belief shall be ours; we have no will but yours. Deign to teach your subjects."

When at last Reuel closed his eyes in slumber, it was with a feeling of greater responsibility and humility than he had ever experienced. Who was he that so high a destiny as lay before him should be thrust upon his shoulders?

*　　*　　*　　*　　*

After these happenings, which we have just recorded, every day Reuel received callers in state. It seemed to him that the entire populace of that great hidden city turned out to do him homage. The Sages, clad in silver armor, attended him as a body-guard, while soldiers and officials high in the councils of the State, were ranged on both sides of the immense hall. The throne on which he sat was a massive one of silver, a bronze Sphinx couched on either side. The steps of the throne were banked with blossoms, offerings from the procession of children that filed slowly by, clad in white, wearing garlands of roses, and laying branches of palm, oleander flowers, lilies and olive sprays before their king.

Offering of gold, silver and gems, silken cloths, priceless articles moulded into unique and exquisite designs, swords of tempered steel, beside which a Damascus blade was coarse and unfinished, filled his artist soul with delight and wonder. Later, Ai escorted him to the underground workshops where brawny smiths plied their trades; and there the secrets of centuries dead and gone were laid bare to his curious gaze.

How was it possible, he asked himself again and again, that a nation so advanced in literature, science and the arts, in the customs of peace and war, could fall as low as had the Ethiopian?

Even while he held the thought, the answer came: As Daniel interpreted Nebuchadnezzar's dream, so has it been and is with Ethiopia. "They shall drive thee from men, and thy dwelling shall be with the beast of the field, and they shall make thee to eat grass as oxen, and they shall wet thee with the dew of heaven, and seven times shall pass over thee, til thou knowest that the Most High ruleth in the kingdom of men, and giveth it to whomsoever He will. Thy kingdom shall be sure unto thee; after that thou shalt have known that the heavens do rule."

But the excitement and changes through which he had passed began to tell upon a constitution already weakened by mental troubles. Ai observed with much concern, the apathy which foretold a serious illness. Hoping to arouse him from painful thoughts which now engrossed his mind, Ai proposed that the visit to the inner city, postponed by the pressure of other duties, be made the next day.

That morning a company, of which the Sages formed a part, started for the inner city. They were to spend the night in travel, resting by day. The progress of the party was very slow, and in a direction Reuel had not yet explored. A deep yellow glow suffused the sky. This soon gave way to the powerful but mellow light of the African moon, casting long shadows over the silvery green of the herbage and foliage. They encountered a perfect network of streams, pursuing their way through virgin forests, brilliant by daylight with beautiful flowers. The woods were inhabited by various kinds of birds of exquisite note and plumage. There were also a goodly number of baboons, who descended from the trees and ranged themselves on the ground to obtain a nearer view of the travellers. They grinned and chattered at the caravan, seeming to regard them as trespassers in their domains.

The character of the country improved as they neared the

interior. Reuel noticed that this was at variance with the European idea respecting Central Africa, which brands these regions as howling wildernesses or an uninhabitable country. He found the landscape most beautiful, the imaginary desert "blossomed like the rose," and the "waste sandy valleys" and "thirsty wilds," which had been assigned to this location became, on close inspection, a gorgeous scene, decorated with Nature's most cheering garniture, teeming with choice specimens of vegetable and animal life, and refreshed by innumerable streams, branches of the rivers, not a few of which were of sufficient magnitude for navigation and commerce. But Reuel remembered the loathsome desert that stood in grim determination guarding the entrance to this paradise against all intrusion, and with an American's practical common sense, bewailed this waste of material.

Proceeding along a mountain gorge, our travellers found the path straitened between the impending mountain on one side and a rapid and sparkling stream on the other. On the opposite side of the ravine the precipices rose abruptly from the very edge of the water. The whole appearance of this mountain pass was singularly grand, romantically wild and picturesquely beautiful. They were often obliged to clamber over huge masses of granite, fallen from the cliffs above; and, on this account, progress was slow and toilsome. On turning an angle of the rock, about the centre of the gorge, the party were suddenly confronted by a huge, tawny lion, which stood directly in the path, with not a wall and scarce a space between. The path was so narrow in this place that it would have been impossible to pass the brute without touching him. Used to the king of the African jungle, the company did not shrink, but faced the animal boldly, although not without some natural physical fear. The lion, too, seemed to be taken by surprise. Thus the opponents stood at a distance of five yards, each staring at the other for several minutes. Had the travellers shown the least signs of fear, or had they attempted to escape, the fate of one, at least, would have been sealed. Now appeared an exhibition of the power of magnetism. Reuel stepped in advance of the foremost bearer, fixed his wonderful and powerful eyes upon the beast, literally transfixing him with a glance, poured the full force of his personal magnetism upon the animal, which almost instantly responded by low growls and an uneasy twisting of the head; finally, the terrible glance remaining inflexible and unwavering, the beast turned himself about and slowly withdrew with a stately and majestic tread, occasionally looking back and uttering a low growl, as if admonishing the travellers to keep their distance.

Murmurs of wonder and admiration broke from Reuel's companions, who were aware of the danger attending the meeting of a hungry lion at close quarters. His admirable intrepidity, and the remarkable powers which were his birthright, had preserved him and his companions.

"Truly, he is the King," they murmured among themselves. And more than ever Ai watched him with increasing love and the fondness of a father.

Without further adventure they reached the portals of the inner city. Their arrival was evidently anticipated, for they were received by a band of young females under the guardianship of a matron. By this escort they were shown to the palace and into the rooms set apart for their reception. Having rested for an hour, bathed and dined, they were ready for the ceremony of introduction. Another guard of women took them in charge, and the procession started down one passage, crossed a great, aislelike hall, and came to a corresponding passage on the other side. On through seemingly endless colonnades they passed, till they came to a huge door formed of great winged creatures. Reuel had thought that nothing could surpass the palace in the outer city for beauty and luxury, but words failed him as his eyes drank in the glories of the lofty apartment into which they stepped, as an Amazon in silver mail threw wide the glittering doors, disclosing the splendor of the royal Presence-chamber. It was a lofty saloon lined with gilded columns, the sunlight falling from the open roof upon the mosaic floor beneath. The tapestries which lined the walls bore exquisite painting of love and warfare.

As the door opened, a voice called. The company halted before a curtained recess, guarded by a group of beautiful girls. Never had Reuel beheld such subtle grace of form and feature, such masses of coal-black hair, such melting eyes of midnight hue. Each girl might have posed for a statue of Venus.

The heavy curtains were lifted now, and discovered the Queen reclining upon a pile of silken cushions—a statue of Venus worked in bronze.

"The Queen is here!" exclaimed a voice. In an instant all present prostrated themselves upon the floor. Reuel alone stood erect, his piercing eyes fixed upon the woman before him.

Grave, tranquil and majestic, surrounded by her virgin guard, she advanced gracefully, bending her haughty head; then, gradually her sinuous body bent and swayed down, down, until she, too, had prostrated herself, and half-knelt, half-lay, upon the marble floor at Reuel's feet.

"O Ergamenes, hast thou indeed returned to thine inheritance?" murmured a voice like unto silver chimes. Reuel started, for it seemed to him that Dianthe's own voice was breathing in his ears.

Knowing now what was expected of him, he raised the Queen with one hand, addressed her courteously in Arabic, led her to her silken couch, seated himself, and would have placed her beside him, but she, with a gesture of dissent, sank upon the cushions at his feet that had served her for footstools.

By this time the Sages had risen and now reclined on the silken couches with which the apartment was well supplied. Ai advanced and addressed the Queen; during this exchange of courtesies, Reuel gazed upon her curiously.

She reminded him strongly of his beautiful Dianthe; in face, the resemblance was so striking that it was painful, and tears, which were no disgrace to his manhood, struggled to his eyes. She was the same height as Dianthe, had the same well-developed shoulders and the same admirable bust. What suppleness in all her movements! What grace, and, at the same time, what strength! Yes; she was a Venus, a superb statue of bronze, moulded by a great sculptor; but an animated statue, in which one saw the blood circulate, and from which life flowed. And what an expressive face, full of character! Long, jet-black hair and totally free, covered her shoulders like a silken mantle; a broad, square forehead, a warm bronze complexion; thick black eyebrows, great black eyes, now soft and languishing—eyes which could weep in sorrow or shoot forth lightning in their anger; a delicate nose with quivering nostrils, teeth of dazzling whiteness behind lips as red as a rose; in her smile of grace and sweetness lurked a sense of power. He was astonished and lost in admiration in spite of himself. Her loveliness was absolutely and ideally perfect. Her attitude of unstudied grace accorded well with the seriousness of her face; she seemed the embodiment of all chastity.

The maidens of her household waited near her—some of them with baskets of flowers upheld in perfect arms. Some brought fruit in glittering dishes and wine in golden goblets of fairy-like fretwork, which were served from stands of ivory and gold. One maiden knelt at her lyre, prepared to strike its chords at pauses in the conversation.

The attendants now retired modestly into the background, while Ai and the other Sages conversed with the Queen. She listened with downcast eyes, occasionally casting a curious, though deferential glance at the muscular figure beside her.

"And dost thou agree, and art thou willing to accept the destiny planned by the Almighty Trinity for thee and me from the beginning of all things, my lord?" she questioned at length in her flute-like voice.

"Queen Candace, thy beauty and graciousness dazzle me. I feel that I can love thee with all my heart; I will fulfill my destiny gladly, and I will cleave to thee until the end."

"Now," answered the Queen with sweet humility, "now, when thou, my lord, doth speak so royally, it doth not become me to lag in generosity." She paused.

Reuel, gazing into her beautiful face, was deeply moved by strong emotions. Again she spoke:

"Behold! in token of submission I bow to my lord, King Ergamenes." She bent herself slowly to the ground, and pressed her knees for one instant upon the mosaic floor. "Behold," and she touched his forehead lightly with her lips, "in earnest of connubial bliss, I kiss thee, King Ergamenes. Behold," and she placed her hand upon his heart, "I swear to thee eternal fealty by the Spirit—the never-changing Trinity." This ceremony ended she seated herself once more beside him. Reuel felt himself yielding readily to her infinite attractiveness. In the azure light and regal splendor of the fragrant apartment, there was rest and satisfaction. All the dreams of wealth and ambition that had haunted the feverish existence by the winding Charles, that had haunted his days of obscure poverty in the halls of Harvard, were about to be realized. Only once had he known joy in his checkered life, and that was when he basked in the society of Dianthe, whom he now designated his spirit-bride. The delirium of that joy had ended in lamentation. Doubts and misgivings had assailed him in the silence of the night when Ai had left him and his influence was withdrawn. Then he had but a faint-hearted belief in the wonderful tale told to him, but here, under Queen Candace's magic influence, all doubts disappeared, and it seemed the most natural thing in the world to be sitting here among these descendants of the ancient Ethiopians, acknowledged as their King, planning a union with a lovely woman, that should give to the world a dynasty of dark-skinned rulers, whose destiny should be to restore the prestige of an ancient people.

Verily, if the wonders he had already seen and heard could be possible in the nineteenth century of progress and enlightenment, nothing was impossible. Dianthe was gone. The world outside held nothing dear to one who had always lived much within himself. The Queen was loving, beautiful—why not accept this pleasant destiny which held its alluring arms so seductively towards him? A sudden moisture filled his eyes; a curious vague softness and tenderness stole over him. Turning abruptly toward his hostess, he held out his own swimming goblet:

"Drink we a loving cup together, oh Queen Candace!" he said in a voice that trembled with earnestness. "I pledge my faith in return for thine!"

The Queen returned his ardent gaze with one of bright surprise and joyous happiness, and bending her head, drank a deep draught of the proffered wine.

"Almost thou lovest me, Ergamenes. May the Eternal Trinity hold fast our bonds!" With a graceful salute she returned the goblet. Reuel drank off in haste what remained within it.

"Behold! I have prepared against this happy hour," continued the Queen, and going to an inlaid cabinet at one side of the room, she took from it a curious ring of dull gold, bearing one priceless gem cut in the form of a lotus lily. "Hold forth thy hand," she said, and on his finger placed the ring.

"Thus do I claim thee for all eternity."

The Sages had watched the actors in this life-drama with jealous eyes that noted every detail with open satisfaction. At Queen Candace's last words, Ai extended his arms with the solemn words:

"And now it is done and never can be undone or altered. Let us hence, that the union may be speedily accomplished."

CHAPTER XVII

 N a month the marriage was to be celebrated with great pomp and rejoicing. Preparations began as soon as the interview between the Queen and the prospective King was over.

After his return from his betrothal, the power of second sight which seemed to have left Reuel for a time, returned in full force. Restlessness was upon him; Dianthe's voice seemed ever calling to him through space. Finally, when his feelings became insupportable, he broached the subject to Ai.

The latter regarded his questioner gravely. "Of a truth thou art a legitimate son of Ethiopia. Thou growest the fruits of wisdom. Descendant of the wise Chaldeans, still powerful to a degree undreamed of by the pigmies of this puny age, you look incredulous, but what I tell you is the solemn truth."

"The Chaldeans disappeared from this world centuries ago," declared Reuel.

"Not all—in me you behold their present head; within this city and the outer world, we still number thousands."

Reuel uttered an exclamation of incredulous amazement. "Not possible!"

Silently Ai went to his cabinet and took down a small, square volume which he placed in Reuel's hand. "It is a record of the wisdom and science of your ancestors."

Reuel turned it over carefully,—the ivory pages were covered with characters sharply defined and finely engraved.

"What language is this? It is not Hebrew, Greek nor Sanskrit, nor any form of hieroglyphic writing."

"It is the language once commonly spoken by your ancestors long before Babylon was builded. It is known to us now as the language of prophecy."

Reuel glanced at the speaker's regal form with admiration and reverence.

"Teach me what thou knowest, Ai," he said humbly, "for, indeed, thou art a wonderful man."

"Gladly," replied Ai, placing his hand in loving tenderness upon the bowed head of the younger man. "Our destiny was foreordained from the beginning to work together for the upbuilding of humanity and the restoration of the race of our fathers. This little book shall teach your soul all that you long to know, and now grasp but vaguely. You believe in the Soul?"

"Most assuredly!"

"As a Personality that continues to live after the body perishes?"

"Certainly."

"And that Personality begins to exert its power over our lives as soon as we begin its cultivation. Death is not necessary to its manifestation upon our lives. There are always angels near! To us who are so blessed and singled out by the Trinity there is a sense of the supernatural always near us—others whom we cannot see, but whose influence is strong upon us in all the affairs of life. Man only proves his ignorance if he denies this fact. Some in the country from which you come contend that the foundations of Christianity are absurd and preposterous, but all the prophecies of the Trinity shall in time be fulfilled. They are working out today by the forces of air, light, wind,—the common things of daily life that pass unnoticed. Ethiopia, too, is stretching forth her hand unto God, and He will fulfill her destiny. The tide of immigration shall set in the early days of the twentieth century, toward Afric's shores, so long bound in the chains of barbarism and idolatry."

Reuel listened entranced, scarce breathing.

"I was warned of your coming long before the knowledge was yours. The day you left your home for New York, I sat within my secret chamber, and all was revealed to me."

"Ay, Ai," Reuel answered, feebly. "But how?"

"You believe that we can hold communion with the living though seas divide and distance is infinite, and our friends who have passed to the future life of light are allowed to comfort us here?"

"I believe."

" 'Tis so," continued Ai. "Half by chance and half by learning, I long ago solved one of the great secrets of Nature. Life is wonderful, but eternity is more wonderful." He paused, regarding affectionately Reuel's troubled face.

"I will answer thy question presently. But can I do aught for thee? Dost memories of that world from which thou hast recently come disturb thee, Ergamenes? I have some feeble powers; if thou wilt, command them." Ai fell into the use of "thee" and "thou" always when greatly moved, and Reuel had become very dear to him.

"I would know some happenings in the world I have left; could my desire be granted, I might, perchance, lose this restlessness which now oppresses me."

Ai regarded him intently. "How far hast thou progressed in knowledge of Infinity?" he asked at length.

"You shall be the judge," replied Reuel. And then ensued a technical conversation on the abstract science of occultism and the future state.

"I see thou are well versed," said Ai finally, evidently well pleased with the young man's versatility. "Come with me. Truly we have not mistaken thee, Ergamenes. Wonderfully hast thou been preserved and fitted for the work before thee."

Reuel had the freedom of the palace, but he knew that there were rooms from which he was excluded. One room especially seemed to be the sanctum sanctorum of the Sages. It was to this room that Ai now conducted him.

Reuel was nearly overpowered with the anticipation of being initiated into the mysteries of this apartment. He found nothing terrifying, however, in the plain, underground room into which he was ushered. A rough table and wooden stools constituted the furniture. The only objects of mystery were a carved table at one end of the apartment, with a silken cloth thrown over its top, and a vessel like a baptismal font, cut in stone, full of water. Air and light came from an outside source, for there were no windows in the room. After closing the door securely, Ai advanced and removed the cloth from the table. "Sit," he commanded. "You ask me how I knew of your coming to my land. Lo, I have followed your career from babyhood. Behold, Ergamenes! What would you see upon the mirror's face? Friend or foe?"

Reuel advanced and looked upon the surface of a disk of which the top of the table was composed. The material of which the polished surface was composed was unknown to Reuel; it was not glass, though quite transparent; it was not metal, though bright as polished steel.

Reuel made no wish, but thought of the spot where the accident had occurred upon the River Charles weeks before. He was startled to observe a familiar scene where he had often rowed for pleasure on pleasant summer evenings. Every minute particular of the scenery was distinctly visible. Presently the water seemed to darken, and he saw distinctly the canoe containing Aubrey,

Molly and Dianthe gliding over the water. He started back aghast, crying out, "It is magical!"

"No, no, Ergamenes, this is a secret of Nature. In this disk I can show thee what thou wilt of the past. In the water of the font we see the future. Think of a face, a scene—I will reflect it for thee on this disk. This is an old secret, known to Ethiopia, Egypt and Arabia centuries ago. I can reflect the past and the faces of those passed away, but the living and the future are cast by the water."

Reuel was awed into silence. He could say nothing, and listened to Ai's learned remarks with a reverence that approached almost to worship before this proof of his supernatural powers. What would the professors of Harvard have said to this, he asked himself. In the heart of Africa was a knowledge of science that all the wealth and learning of modern times could not emulate. For some time the images came and went upon the mirror, in obedience to his desires. He saw the scenes of his boyhood, the friends of his youth, and experienced anew the delights of life's morning. Then he idly desired to see the face of his loved Dianthe, as she last appeared on earth. The surface of the disk reflected nothing!

"You have not reached perfection then, in this reflector?"

"Why think you so?" asked Ai gravely.

"I have asked to see the face of a friend who is dead. The mirror did not reflect it."

"The disk cannot err," said Ai. "Let us try the water in the font."

"But that reflects the living, you say; she is dead."

"The disk cannot err," persisted Ai. He turned to the font, gazed in its surface, and then beckoned Reuel to approach. From the glassy surface Dianthe's face gazed back at him, worn and lined with grief.

" 'Tis she!" he cried, "her very self."

"Then your friend still lives," said Ai, calmly.

"Impossible!"

"Why do you doubt my word, Ergamenes?"

Then with great suppressed excitement and much agitation, Reuel repeated the story of Dianthe's death as brought to him by the last mail he had received from America.

"You say that 'Molly,' as you call her, was also drowned?"

"Yes."

"Let us try the disk."

They returned to the mirror and instantly the face of Molly Vance gazed at them from the river's bed, surrounded by seaweed and grasses.

"Can a man believe in his own sanity!" exclaimed Reuel in an agony of perplexity.

Ai made no reply, but returned to the font. "I think it best to call up the face of your enemy. I am sure you have one." Immediately the water reflected the debonair face of Aubrey Livingston, which was almost instantly blotted out by the face of Jim Titus.

"Two!" murmured Ai. "I thought so."

"If she then lives, as your science seems to insist, show me her present situation," cried Reuel, beside himself with fears.

"I must have a special preparation for the present," said Ai, calmly. He set about preparing a liquid mixture. When this was accomplished he washed the face of the disk with a small sponge dipped in the mixture. A film of sediment instantly formed upon it.

"When this has dried, I will scrape it off and polish the mirror, then we shall be ready for the demonstration. One picture only will come—this will remain for a number of days, after that the disk will return to its normal condition. But, see! the sediment is caked. Now to remove it and finish our test." At last it was done, and the disk repolished. Then standing before it, Ai cried, in an earnest voice:

"Let the present appear upon the disk, if it be for the benefit of Thy human subjects!"

Ai appeared perfectly calm, but his hands shook. Reuel remained a short remove from him, awaiting his summons.

"Come, Ergamenes."

For a few moments Reuel gazed upon the plate, his eyes, brilliant with expectation, his cheeks aglow with excitement. Then he involuntarily shuddered, a half suppressed groan escaped him, and he grew ashy pale. In a trice he became entirely unnerved, and staggered back and forth like a drunken man. Greatly alarmed, and seeing he was about to fall, Ai sprang to his side and caught him. Too late. He fell to the floor in a swoon. The picture reflected by the disk was that of the ancestral home of the Livingstons. It showed the parlor of a fine old mansion; two figures stood at an open window, their faces turned to the interior. About the woman's waist the man's arm was twined in a loving embrace. The faces were those of Aubrey and Dianthe.

Late that night Reuel tossed upon his silken couch in distress of mind. If the disk were true, then Dianthe and Aubrey both lived and were together. He was torn by doubts, haunted by dreadful fears of he knew not what. If the story of the disk were true, never was man so deceived and duped as he had been. Then in the midst of his anger and despair came an irresistible impulse to rise from his bed. He did so, and distinctly felt the pressure of a soft hand upon his brow, and a yielding body at his side. The next instant he could have sworn that he heard the well-known tones of Dianthe in his ears, saying:

"Reuel, it is I."

Unable to answer, but entirely conscious of a presence near him, he had presence of mind enough to reiterate a mental question. His voiceless question was fully understood, for again the familiar voice spoke:

"I am not dead, my husband; but I am lost to you. Not of my own seeking has this treachery been to thee, O beloved. The friend into whose care you gave me has acquired the power over me that you alone possessed, the power sacred to our first meeting and our happy love. Why did you leave me in the power of a fiend in human shape, to search for gold? There are worse things in life than poverty."

Calming the frenzy of his thoughts by a strong effort, Reuel continued his mental questions until the whole pitiful story was his. He knew not how long he continued in this communion. Over and over he turned the story he had learned in the past few hours. Ungovernable rage against his false friend possessed him. "Blind, fool, dupe, dotard!" he called himself, not to have seen the treachery beneath the mask of friendship. And then to leave her helpless in the hands of this monster, who had not even spared his own betrothed to compass his love for another.

But at least revenge was left him. He would return to America and confront Aubrey Livingston with his guilt. But how to get away from the hidden city. He knew that virtually he was a prisoner.

Still turning over ways and means, he fell into an uneasy slumber, from which he was aroused by a dreadful shriek.

CHAPTER XVIII

T was now two months since Reuel's strange disappearance from the camp of the explorers. Day after day they had searched every inch of the ground within and about the pyramids, with no success. Charlie Vance was inconsolable, and declared his intention of making his home at Meroe until Reuel was found. He scouted the idea of his death by falling a prey to wild beasts, and hung about the vicinity of the Great Pyramid with stubborn persistence. He was no longer the spoiled darling of wealth and fashion, but a serious-minded man of a taciturn disposition.

He spent money like water in his endeavor to find the secret passage, believing that it existed, and that in it Reuel was lost.

One morning he and Jim Titus laid bare a beautifully worked marble wall, built of fine masonry, with even blocks, each a meter and a half long, and below the exquisitely worked moulding two further layers of well-worked calcareous stone. The whole formed a foundation for a structure which had fallen into ruins about two and a half meters high. But this wall continued for thirteen meters only, and then returned at right angles at each end. On the inner side this marble structure was backed by large blocks of calcareous stone, and in the inner angles, they had with much labor to break up and remove two layers of block superimposed at right angles, one upon another. The entire party was much puzzled to learn what this structure could have been.

Sculptures and paintings lined the walls. As usual, there was a queen, attired in a long robe. The queen had in one hand the lash of Osiris and in the other a lotus flower.

At the extremity of each portico was the representation of a monolithic temple, above which were the traces of a funeral boat filled with figures.

After two days' work, the skilled diggers assured the explorers that they could do nothing with the debris but to leave it, as it was impossible to open the structure. But in the night, Charlie was kept awake by the thought that this curious structure might hold the expedition's secret; and remembering that perseverance was never beaten, set to work there the next morning, digging into the interior and breaking up the huge blocks which impeded his progress. The next day another impediment was reached, and it was decided to give it up. Again Charlie was awake all night, puzzling over the difficulties encountered, and again he made up his mind not to give it up. Charlie was learning many needed lessons in bitterness of spirit out in these African wilds. Sorrow had come to him here in the loss of his sister, and the disappearance of his friend. As Reuel had done in the night weeks before, so he did now, rising and dressing and securing his weapons, but taking the precaution to awaken Jim, and ask him to accompany him for a last visit to the Pyramid.

Jim Titus seemed strangely subdued and quiet since Reuel's disappearance. Charlie decided that their suspicions were wrong, and that Jim was a good fellow, after all.

As they trudged along over the sandy paths in the light of the great African moon, Charlie was glad of Jim's lively conversation. Anecdotes of Southern life flowed glibly from his tongue, illustrated by songs descriptive of life there. It really seemed to Vance that a portion of the United States had been transported to Africa.

They entered the great Pyramid, as Reuel had done before them, lit their torches, and began slowly and carefully to go over the work of excavation already done.

They passed down a side passage opening out of the outer passage, made a number of steps and along an underground shaft made by the workmen. Suddenly the passage ended. They halted, held up the lamps and saw such a scene as they were not likely to see again. They stood on the edge of an enormous pit, hedged in by a wall of rock. There was an opening in the wall, made by a hinged block of stone. This solid door had opened noiselessly, dark figures had stolen forth, and had surrounded the two men. As they discovered their strange companions, weapons of burnished steel flashed and seemed to fill the vault. Not a sound was heard but the deep breathing of men in grim determination and on serious business bent. Instantly the two travelers were bound and gagged.

*   *   *   *   *

Instantly, after the seizure, the eyes of the prisoners were blindfolded; then they were half led, half dragged along by their captors. As he felt the grip of steel which impelled a forward movement, Charlie bitterly cursed his own folly in undertaking so mad a venture. "Poor Reuel," he lamented, "was this the explanation of his disappearance?" Reuel had been the life of the party; next to Professor Stone, he was looked up to as leader and guide, and with his loss, all interest seemed to have dropped from the members of the expedition.

For half an hour they were hurried along what must have been deep underground passages. Charlie could feel the path drop beneath his feet on solid rock which seemed to curve over like the edges of a waterfall. He stumbled, and would have fallen if strong arms had not upheld him. He could feel the rock worn into deep gutters smoother than ice. For the first time he heard the sound of his captors' voices. One in command gave an order in an unknown tongue. Charlie wished then that he had spent more time in study and less in sport.

"Oh," he groaned in spirit, "what a predicament for a free-born American citizen, and one who has had on the gloves with many a famous ring champion!" He wondered how Jim was far-ing, for since the first frightened yell from his lips, all had been silence.

There came another brief command in the unknown tongue, and the party halted. Then Charlie felt himself lifted into what he finally determined was a litter. He settled himself comfortably, and the bearers started. Charlie was of a philosophical nature; if he had been poor and forced to work for a living, he might have become a learned philosopher. So he lay and reflected, and won-dered whether this experience would end, until, lulled by the yielding motion and the gentle swaying, he fell asleep.

He must have slept many hours, for when he awoke he felt a strong sensation of hunger. They were still journeying at a leisurely pace. Charlie could feel the sweet, fresh air in his face, and could hear the song of birds, and smell the scented air, heavy with the fragrance of flowers and fruits. Mentally thanking God that he still lived, he anxiously awaited the end of this strange journey. Presently he felt that they entered a building, for the current of air ceased, and the soft footsteps of the bearers gave forth a metallic sound. There came another command in the unknown tongue, and the bearers stopped; he was told to descend, in unmistakable English, by a familiar voice. He obeyed the voice, and instantly he was relieved of his bandage; before his sight became accustomed to the semi-darkness of the room, he heard the retreating steps of a number of men. As his sight returned in full, he saw before him Ai and Abdallah and Jim.

Abdallah regarded him with a gaze that was stolid and

unrecognizing. The room in which he stood was large and circular. Floors and walls were of the whitest marble, and from the roof light and air were supplied. There were two couches in the room, and a divan ran about one of its sides. There was no door or entrance visible—nothing but the unvarying white walls and flooring.

"Stranger," said Ai, in his mellow voice, speaking English in fluent tones, "Why hast thou dared to uncover the mysteries of centuries? Art thou weary of life that thou hast dared to trifle with Nature's secrets? Scarce an alien foot has traversed this land since six thousand years have passed. Art weary of living?" As he asked the last question, Charlie felt a chill of apprehension. This man, with his strange garb, his dark complexion, his deep eyes and mystic smile, was to be feared and reverenced. Summoning up all his sangfroid and determination not to give in to his fears, he replied,—

"We came to find old things, that we may impart our knowledge to the people of our land, who are eager to know the beginning of all things. I come of a race bold and venturesome, who know not fear if we can get a few more dollars and fresh information."

"I have heard of your people," replied Ai, with a mysterious sparkle in his eyes. "They are the people who count it a disgrace to bear my color; is it not so?"

"Great Scott!" thought Charlie, turning mental somersaults to find an answer that would placate the dignitary before him. "Is it possible that the ubiquitous race question has got ahead of the expedition! By mighty, it's time something was done to stop this business. Talk of Banquo's ghost! Banquo ain't in it if this is the race question I'm up against." Aloud he said, "My venerable and esteemed friend, you could get there all right with your complexion in my country. We would simply label you 'Arab,

Turk, Malay or Filipino,' and in that costume you'd slide along all right; not the slightest trouble when you showed your ticket at the door. Savee?" He finished with a profound bow.

Ai eyed him sadly for a moment, and then said,—

"O, flippant-tongued offspring of an ungenerous people, how is it with my brother?" and he took Jim's unresisting hand and led him up to Charlie. "Crisp of hair," and he passed his hand softly over Jim's curly pate. "Black of skin! How do you treat such as this one in your country?"

Charlie felt embarrassed in spite of his assurance. "Well, of course, it has been the custom to count Africans as our servants, and they have fared as servants."

"And yet, ye are all of one blood; descended from one common father. Is there ever a flock or herd without its black member? What more beautiful than the satin gloss of the raven's wing, the soft litter of eyes of blackest tint or the rich black fur of your own native animals? Fair-haired worshippers of Mammon, do you not know that you have been weighed in the balance and found wanting? that your course is done? that Ethiopia's bondage is about over, her travail passed?"

Charlie smiled in inward mirth at what he called the "fossilized piece of antiquity." "Touched in the forehead; crank," was his mental comment. "I'd better put on the brakes, and not aggravate this lunatic. He's probably some kind of a king, and might make it hot for me." Aloud he said, "Pardon, Mr. King, but what has this to do with making me a prisoner? Why have I been brought here?"

"You will know soon enough," replied Ai, as he clapped his hands. Abdallah moved to the side of the room, and instantly a marble block slid from its position, through which Ai and he departed, leaving the prisoners alone.

For a while the two men sat and looked at each other in

helpless silence. Then Jim broke the silence with lamentations.

"Oh, Lord! Mr. Vance, there's a hoodoo on this business, and I'm the hoodoo!"

"Nonsense!" exclaimed Vance. "Be a man, Jim, and help me find a way out of this infernal business."

But Jim sat on the divan, lamenting and refusing to be comforted. Presently food was brought to them, and then after many and useless conjectures, they lay down and tried to sleep.

The night passed very comfortably on the whole, although the profound silence was suggestive of being buried alive. Another day and night passed without incident. Food was supplied them at regular intervals. Charlie's thoughts were varied. He—fastidious and refined—who had known no hardship and no sorrow,—why had he left his country to wander among untutored savages? None were there to comfort him of all his friends. These walls would open but to admit the savage executioner. He ground his teeth. He thought of Cora Scott; doubtless she thought him dead. Dead! No; nor would he die. He'd find a way out of this or perish; he'd go home and marry Cora. Now this was a most surprising conclusion, for Charlie had been heard to say many times that "he'd be drawn and quartered before he'd tie up to a girl of the period," which Cora undoubtedly was. As if aroused from a dream, he jumped up and going over to Jim, shook him. The Negro turned uneasily in his sleep and groaned. Again he shook him.

"Get up, Jim. Come, I'm going to try to get out of this."

"I'm afraid, Mr. Vance; it's no use."

"Come on, Jim; be a man."

"I'm ready for anything, only show me the way," replied Jim in desperation. Their pistols had been taken from them, but their knives remained. They stored what food remained about their persons and began a thorough examination of the room.

"They certainly find an exit here somewhere, Jim, and we must find it too."

"Easier said than done, I fear, sir."

An hour—two hours, passed in fruitless search; the marble walls showed not a sign of exit or entrance. They rested then, sitting on the sides of the divans and gazing at each other in utter helplessness. The full moonlight showered the apartment with a soft radiance from the domed roof. Suddenly, Jim sprang forward and inserted his knife in a crevice in the floor. Instantly Charlie was beside him, working like mad on the other side. The slab began to waver to and fro, as though shaken by a strong force—the crack widened—they saw a round, flat metal button—Jim seized it with one hand and pried with the knife in the other—a strong breeze of subterranean air struck through the narrow opening—and with a dull reverberation half the flooring slid back, revealing what seemed to be a vast hole.

The men recoiled, and lay panting from their labors on the edges of the subway. Charlie blessed his lucky stars that hidden in his clothes was a bundle of tapers used by the explorers for just such emergencies. By great good fortune, his captors had not discovered them.

"What's to be done now, Jim?"

"Get down there and explore, but hanged if I want the job, Mr. Vance."

"We'll go together, Jim. Let's see," he mused, "What did Prof. Stone's parchment say? 'Beware the tank to the right where dwells the sacred crocodile, still living, although centuries have rolled by, and men have been gathered to the shades who once tended on his wants. And beware the fifth gallery to the right where abide the sacred serpents with jewelled crowns, for of a truth are they terrible," quoted Charlie, dreamily.

"You don't suppose this is the place you were hunting for, do you?" queried Jim, with eyes big with excitement.

"Jim, my boy, that's a question no man can answer at this distance from the object of our search. But if it is, as I suspect, the way to the treasure will lead us to liberty, for the other end must be within the pyramid. I'm for searching this passage. Come on if you are with me."

He lighted his taper and swung it into the abyss, disclosing steps of granite leading off in the darkness. As his head disappeared from view, Jim, with a shudder, followed. The steps led to a passage or passages, for the whole of the underground room was formed of vaulted passages, sliding off in every direction. The stairs ended in another passage; the men went down it; it was situated, as nearly as they could judge, directly beneath the room where they had been confined. Silently the two figures crept on, literally feeling their way. Shortly they came to another passage running at right angles; slowly they crept along the tunnel, for it was nothing more, narrowing until it suddenly ended in a sort of cave, running at right angles, they crossed this, halting at the further side to rest and think. Charlie looked anxiously about him for signs, but saw nothing alarming in the smooth sandy floor, and irregular contorted sides. The floor was strewn with bowlders like the bed of a torrent. As they went on, the cavern widened into an ampitheatre with huge supporting columns. To the right and left of the cave there were immense bare spaces stretching away into immense galleries. Here they paused to rest, eating sparingly of the food they had brought. "Let us rest here," said Charlie, "I am dead beat."

"Is it not safer to go on? We cannot be very far from the room where we were confined."

"I'll sit here a few moments, anyhow," replied Charlie. Jim

wandered aimlessly about the great vault, turning over stones and peering into crevices.

"What do you expect to find, Jim, the buried treasure?" laughed Charlie, as he noted the earnestness of the other's search.

Jim was bending over something—wrenching off a great iron cover. Suddenly he cried out, "Mr. Vance, here it is!"

Charlie reached his side with a bound. There sat Jim, and in front of him lay, imbedded in the sand of the cavern's floor, a huge box, long and wide and deep, whose rusted hinges could not withstand the stalwart Negro's frantic efforts.

With a shuddering sigh the lid was thrust back, falling to one side with a great groan of almost mortal anguish as it gave up the trust committed to its care ages before. They both gazed, and as they gazed were well-nigh blinded. For this is what they saw:—

At first, a blaze of darting rays that sparkled out and shot out myriad scintillations of color—red, violet, orange, green, and deepest crimson. Then by degrees, they saw that these hues came from a jumbled heap of gems—some large, some small, but together in value beyond all dreams of wealth.

Diamonds, rubies, sapphires, amethysts, opals, emeralds, turquoises—lay roughly heaped together, some polished, some uncut, some as necklaces and chains, others gleaming in rings and bracelets—wealth beyond the dreams of princes.

Near to the first box lay another, and in it lay gold in bars and gold in flakes, hidden by the priests of Osiris, that had adorned the crowns of queens Candace and Semiramis—a spectacle glorious beyond compare.

"The Professor's parchment told the truth," cried Charlie, after a few moments, when he had regained his breath. "But what shall we do with it, now we have it?" asked Jim in disconsolate tones. "We can't carry it with us."

"True for you, Jim," replied Vance, sadly. "This wealth is a mockery now we have it. Jim, we're left, badly left. Here we've been romping around for almost six months after this very treasure, and now we've got it we can't hold it. This whole expedition has been like monkeying with a saw mill, Jim, my boy, and I for one, give in beaten. Left, I should say so; badly left, when I counted Africa a played-out hole in the ground. And, Jim, when we get home, if we ever do, the drinks are on me. Now, old man, stow some of these glittering baubles in your clothing, as I am going to do, and then we'll renew our travels." He spoke in jest, but the tears were in his eyes, and as he clasped Jim's toil-hardened black hand, he told himself that Ai's words were true. Where was the color line now? Jim was a brother; the nearness of their desolation in this uncanny land, left nothing but a feeling of brotherhood. He felt then the truth of the words, "Of one blood have I made all races of men."

As they stooped to replace the cover, Jim's foot knocked against an iron ring set in the sandy flooring. "I believe it's another box, Mr. Vance," he called out, and dropping his work, he pulled with all his might.

"Careful, Jim," called Charlie's warning voice. Too late! The ring disappeared at the second tug, revealing a black pit from which came the odor of musk. From out the darkness came the sweeping sound of a great body moving in wavelets over a vast space. Fascinated into perfect stillness, Vance became aware of pale emerald eyes watching him, and the sound of deep breathing other than their own. There was a wild rattle and rush in the darkness, as Jim, moving forward, flung down his taper and turned to flee.

"The serpents! the serpents! Fly for your life, Jim!" shouted Charlie, as he dashed away from the opening. Too late! There came a terrible cry, repeated again and again. Charlie Vance sunk upon the ground, overcome with horror.

CHAPTER XIX

T must have been about one o'clock in the morning when Reuel started out of a fitful slumber by the sound of that terrible scream. He sprang to his feet and listened. He heard not a sound; all was silence within the palace. But his experience was so vivid that reason could not control his feelings; he threw wide the dividing curtains, and fled out upon the balcony. All was silence. The moonlight flooded the landscape with the strength of daylight. As he stood trying to calm himself, a shadow fell across his path, and raising his eyes, he beheld the form of Mira; she beckoned him on, and he, turning, followed the shadowy figure, full of confidence that she would show him the way to that fearful scream.

On they glided like two shadows, until the phantom paused before what seemed a solid wall, and with warning gaze and uplifted finger, bade him enter. It was a portion of the palace unfamiliar to him; the walls presented no hope of entrance. What could it mean? Mira faded from his gaze, and as he stood there puzzling over this happening, suddenly the solid wall began to glide away, leaving a yawning space, in which appeared Ai's startled and disturbed face.

"Back!" he cried, as he beheld his King. "Back, Ergamenes! how come you here?"

"What was the cry I heard, Ai? I cannot rest. I have been led hither," he continued, significantly. Then, noticing the other's disturbed vision, he continued, "Tell me. I command you."

With a murmured protest, Ai stepped aside, saying, "Perhaps it is best."

Reuel advanced into the room. The hole in the floor was securely closed, and on the divans lay Charlie Vance, white and unconscious, and Jim Titus, crushed almost to a jelly but still alive. Abdallah and a group of natives were working over Vance, trying to restore consciousness. Reuel gave one startled, terrified glance at the two figures, and staggered backward to the wall.

Upon hearing that cry, Jim Titus stirred uneasily, and muttered, "It's him!"

"He wishes to speak with you," said Ai, gravely.

"How came they here, and thus?" demanded Reuel in threatening anger.

"They were searching for you, and we found them, too, in the pyramid. We confined them here, debating what was best to do, fearing you would become dissatisfied. They tried to escape and found the treasure and the snakes. The black man will die."

"Are you there, Mr. Reuel?" came in a muffled voice from the dying man.

Reuel stood beside him and took his hand,—"Yes, Jim, it is I; how came you thus?"

"The way of the transgressor is hard," groaned the man. "I would not have been here had I not consented to take your life. I am sure you must have suspected me; I was but a bungler, and often my heart failed me."

"Unhappy man! how could you plot to hurt one who has never harmed you?" exclaimed Reuel.

"Aubrey Livingston was my foster brother, and I could deny him nothing."

"Aubrey Livingston! Was he the instigator?"

"Yes," sighed the dying man. "Return home as soon as pos-

sible and rescue your wife—your wife, and yet not your wife—
for a man may not marry his sister."

"What!" almost shrieked Reuel. "What!"

"I have said it. Dianthe Lusk is your own sister, the half-
sister of Aubrey Livingston, who is your half-brother."

Reuel stood for a moment, apparently struggling for words
to answer the dying man's assertion, then fell on his knees in a
passion of sobs agonizing to witness. "You know then, Jim, that
I am Mira's son?" he said at length.

"I do. Aubrey planned to have Miss Dianthe from the first
night he saw her; he got you this chance with the expedition; he
kept you from getting anything else to force you to a separation
from the girl. He bribed me to accidentally put you out of the way.
He killed Miss Molly to have a free road to Dianthe. Go home,
Reuel Briggs, and at least rescue the girl from misery. Watch,
watch, or he will outwit you yet." Reuel started in a frenzy of rage
to seize the man, but Ai's hand was on his arm.

"Peace, Ergamenes; he belongs to the ages now."

One more convulsive grasp, and Jim Titus had gone to
atone for the deeds done in the flesh.

With pallid lips and trembling frame, Reuel turned from the
dead to the living. As he sat beside his friend, his mind was far
away in America looking with brooding eyes into the past and
gazing hopelessly into the future. Truly hath the poet said,—

"The evil that men do lives after them."

And Reuel cursed with a mighty curse the bond that bound
him to the white race of his native land.

*   *   *   *   *

One month after the events narrated in the previous chapter, a
strange party stood on the deck of the out-going steamer at

Alexandria, Egypt—Reuel and Charlie Vance, accompanied by Ai and Abdallah in the guise of servants. Ai had with great difficulty obtained permission of the Council to allow King Ergamenes to return to America. This was finally accomplished by Ai's being surety for Reuel's safe return, and so the journey was begun which was to end in the apprehension and punishment of Aubrey Livingston.

Through the long journey homeward two men thought only of vengeance, but with very different degrees of feeling. Charlie Vance held to the old Bible punishment for the pure crime of manslaughter, but in Reuel's wrongs lay something beyond the reach of punishment by the law's arm; in it was the accumulation of years of foulest wrongs heaped upon the innocent and defenseless women of a race, added to this last great outrage. At night he said, as he paced the narrow confines of the deck, "Thank God, it is night;" and when the faint streaks of dawn glowed in the distance, gradually creeping across the expanse of waters, "Thank God, it is morning." Another hour, and he would say, "Would God it were night!" By day or night some phantom in his ears holloes in ocean's roar or booms in thunder, howls in the winds or murmurs in the breeze, chants in the voice of the sea-fowl—"Too late, too late. 'Tis done, and worse than murder."

Westward the vessel sped—westward while the sun showed only as a crimson ball in its Arabian setting, or gleamed through a veil of smoke off the English coast, ending in the grey, angry, white-capped waves of the Atlantic in winter.

CHAPTER XX

T was believed by the general public and Mr. Vance that Molly and Dianthe had perished beneath the waters of the Charles River, although only Molly's body was recovered. Aubrey was picked up on the bank of the river in an unconscious state, where he was supposed to have made his way after vainly striving to rescue the two girls.

When he had somewhat recovered from the shock of the accident, it was rumored that he had gone to Canada with a hunting party, and so he disappeared from public view.

But Dianthe had not perished. As the three struggled in the water, Molly, with all the confidence of requited love, threw her arms about her lover. With a muttered oath, Aubrey tried to shake her off, but her clinging arms refused to release him. From the encircling arms he saw a sight that maddened him—Dianthe's head was disappearing beneath the waters where the lily-stems floated in their fatal beauty, holding in their tenacious grasp the girl he loved. An appalling sound had broken through the air as she went down—a heart-stirring cry of agony—the tone of a voice pleading with God for life! the precious boon of life! That cry drove away the man, and the brute instinct so rife within us all, ready always to leap to the front in times of excitement or danger, took full possession of the body. He forgot honor, humanity, God.

With a savage kick he freed himself and swam swiftly toward the spot where Dianthe's golden head had last appeared.

He was just in time. Grasping the flowing locks with one hand and holding her head above the treacherous water, he swam with her to the bank.

Pretty, innocent, tender-hearted Molly sank never to rise again. Without a word, but with a look of anguished horror, her despairing face was covered by the glistening, greedy waters that lapped so hungrily about the water-lily beds.

As Aubrey bore Dianthe up the bank his fascinated gaze went backward to the spot where he had seen Molly sink. To his surprise and horror, as he gazed the body rose to the surface and floated as did poor Elaine:

> *"In her right hand the lily,*
> *—All her bright hair streaming down—*
> *—And she herself in white,*
> *All but her face, and that clear-featured face*
> *Was lovely, for she did not seem as dead,*
> *But fast asleep, and lay as tho' she smiled."*

Staggering like a drunken man, he made his way to a small cottage up the bank, where a woman, evidently expecting him, opened the door without waiting for his knock.

"Quick! here she is. Not a word. I will return tonight." With these words Livingston sped back to the river bank, where he was found by the rescuing party, in a seemingly exhausted condition.

For weeks after these happenings Dianthe lived in another world, unconscious of her own identity. It was early fall before her full faculties were once more with her. The influence which Livingston had acquired rendered her quiescent in his hands, and not too curious as to circumstances of time and place. One day he brought her a letter, stating that Reuel was dead.

Sick at heart, bending beneath the blight that thus unexpectedly fell upon her, the girl gave herself up to grief, and weary of the buffets of Fate, yielded to Aubrey's persuasions and became his wife. On the night which witnessed Jim Titus's awful death, they had just returned to Livingston's ancestral home in Maryland.

It would be desecration to call the passion which Aubrey entertained for Dianthe, love. Yet passion it was—the greatest he had ever known—with its shadow, jealousy. Indifference on the part of his idol could not touch him; she was his other self, and he hated all things that stood between him and his love.

It was a blustering night in the first part of November. It was twilight. Within the house profound stillness reigned. The heavens were shut out of sight by masses of sullen, inky clouds, and a piercing north wind was howling. Within the room where Dianthe lay, a glorious fire burnt in a wide, low grate. A table, a couch and some chairs were drawn near to it for warmth. Dianthe lay alone. Presently there came a knock at the door. "Enter," said the pale woman on the couch, never once removing her gaze from the whirling flakes and sombre sky.

Aubrey entered and stood for some moments gazing in silence at the beautiful picture presented to his view. She was gowned in spotless white, her bright hair flowed about her unconstrained by comb or pin. Her features were like marble, the deep grey eyes gazed wistfully into the far distance. The man looked at her with hungry, devouring eyes. Something, he knew not what, had come between them. His coveted happiness, sin-bought and crime-stained, had turned to ashes— Dead-Sea fruit indeed. The cold gaze she turned on him half froze him, and changed his feelings into a corresponding channel with her own.

"You are ill, Dianthe. What seems to be your trouble? I am

told that you see spirits. May I ask if they wear the dress of African explorers?".

It had come to this unhappy state between them.

"Aubrey," replied the girl in a calm, dispassionate tone, "Aubrey, at this very hour in this room, as I lay here, not sleeping, nor disposed to sleep there where you stand, stood a lovely woman; I have seen her thus once before. She neither looked at me nor spoke, but walked to the table, opened the Bible, stooped over it a while, seeming to write, then seemed to sink, just as she rose, and disappeared. Examine the book, and tell me, is that fancy?"

Crossing the room, Aubrey gazed steadfastly at the open book. It was the old family Bible, and the heavy clasps had grown stiff and rusty. It was familiar to him, and intimately associated with his life-history. There on the open page were ink lines underscoring the twelfth chapter of Luke: "For there is nothing covered that shall not be revealed, neither hid that shall not be known." At the end of this passage was written the one word "Nina" ["Mira"?].

Without a comment, but with anxious brows, Aubrey returned to his wife's couch, stooped and impressed several kisses on her impassive face. Then he left the room.

Dianthe lay in long and silent meditation. Servants came and went noiselessly. She would have no candles. The storm ceased; the moon came forth and flooding the landscape, shone through the windows upon the lonely watcher. Dianthe's restlessness was soothed, and she began tracing the shadows on the carpet and weaving them into fantastic images of imagination. What breaks her reverie? The moonlight gleams on something white and square; it is a letter. She left the couch and picked it up. Just then a maid entered with a light, and she glanced at the envelope. It bore the African postmark! She paused. Then as the girl left the room, she slipped the letter from the envelope and read:

> *"Master Aubrey,—I write to inform you that I have not been able to comply with your wishes. Twice I have trapped Dr. Briggs, but he has escaped miraculously from my hands. I shall not fail the third time. The expedition will leave for Meroe next week, and then something will surely happen. I have suppressed all letters, according to your orders, and both men are feeling exceedingly blue. Kindly put that first payment on the five thousand dollars to my sister's credit in a Baltimore bank, and let her have the bank book. Next mail you may expect something definite.*
>
>

"Yours faithfully,
"Jim Titus."

Aubrey Livingston had gone to an adjoining city on business, and would be absent three or four days.

That night Dianthe spent in his library behind locked doors, and all about her lay open letters—letters addressed to her, and full of love and tenderness, detailing Reuel's travels and minutely describing every part of his work.

Still daylight found her at her work. Then she quitted it, closed up the desk, tied up the letters, replaced them, left the room, and returned to her boudoir to think. Her brain was in a giddy whirl, and but one thought stood out clearly in her burning brain. Her thoughts took shape in the one word "Reuel," and by her side stood again the form of the pale, lovely mulattress, her long black curls enveloping her like a veil. One moment—the next the room was vacant save for herself.

Reuel was living, and she a bigamist—another's wife! made so by fraud and deceit. The poor overwrought brain was working like a machine now—throbbing, throbbing, throbbing. To see him, hear his voice—this would be enough. Then came the thought—lost to her, or rather she to him—and how? By the plans of this would-be murderer. O, horrible, inhuman wretch! He had stolen her by false tales, and then had polluted her existence by the breath of murder. Murder! What was murder? She paused and grasped for breath; then came the trembling thought, "Would he were dead!"

He would return and discover the opening of the letters. "O, that he were dead!"

She wandered about the grounds in the cold sunshine, burning with fever, and wild with a brain distraught. She wished the trees were living creatures and would fall and crush him. The winds in their fury, would they but kill him! O, would not something aid her? At last she sat down, out of breath with her wanderings and wearied by the tumult within her breast. So it went all day; the very heavens beckoned her to commit a deed of horror. She slept and dreamed of shapeless, nameless things that lurked and skulked in hidden chambers, waiting the signal to come forth. She woke and slept no more. She turned and turned the remainder of the night; her poor warped faculties recalled the stories she had read of Cenci, the Borgias, and even the Hebrew Judith. And then she thought of Reuel, and the things he had told her on many an idle day, of the properties of medicine, and how in curiosity she had fingered his retorts used in experiments. And he had told her she was apt, and he would teach her many things of his mysterious profession. And as she thought and speculated, suddenly something whispered, as it were, a name—heard but once—in her ear. It was the name of a poison so subtle in its action as to defy detection save by one versed in its use. With a shudder she threw the thought from her, and rose from her couch.

We know we're tempted. The world is full of precedents, the air with impulses, society with men and spirit tempters. But what invites sin? Is it not a something within ourselves? Are we not placed here with a sinful nature which the plan of salvation commands us to overcome? If we offer the excuse that we were tempted, where is the merit of victory if we do not resist the tempter? God does not abandon us to evil prompters without a white-robed angel, stretching out a warning hand and pointing out the better way as strongly as the other. When we conquer sin, we say we are virtuous, triumphant, and when we fall, we excuse our sins by saying, "It is fate."

The days sped on. To the on-looker life jogged along as monotonously at Livingston Hall as in any other quiet home. The couple dined and rode, and received friends in the conventional way. Many festivities were planned in honor of the beautiful bride. But, alas! these days but goaded her to madness. The uncertainty of Reuel's fate, her own wrongs as a wife yet not a wife, her husband's agency in all this woe, the frailness of her health, weighed more and more upon a mind weakened by hypnotic experiments. Her better angel whispered still, and she listened until one day there was a happening that turned the scale, and she pronounced her own dreadful doom— "For me there's no retreat."

CHAPTER XXI

T was past midday about two weeks later that Dianthe wandered about the silent woods, flitting through the mazes of unfamiliar forest paths. Buried in sad thoughts she was at length conscious that her surroundings were strange, and that she had lost her way. Every now and then the air was thick and misty with powdery flakes of snow which fell, or swept down, rather, upon the brown leaf-beds and withered grass. The buffeting winds which kissed her glowing hair into waving tendrils brought no color to her white cheeks and no light to her eyes. For days she had been like this, thinking only of getting away from the busy house with its trained servants and its loathsome luxury which stifled her. How to escape the chains which bound her to this man was now her only thought. If Reuel lived, each day that found her still beneath the roof of this man whose wife she was in the eyes of the world, was a crime. Away, away, looking forward to she knew not what, only to get away from the sight of his hated face.

Presently she paused and looked about her. Where was she? The spot was wild and unfamiliar. There was no sight or sound of human being to question as to the right direction to take, not that it mattered much, she told herself in bitterness of spirit. She walked on more slowly now, scanning the woods for signs of a human habitation. An opening in the trees gave a glimpse of cultivated ground in a small clearing, and a few steps farther revealed a typical Southern Negro cabin, from which a woman stepped out and faced her as if expecting her coming. She was very aged, but still erect and noble in form. The patched figure was neat to scrupulousness, the eye still keen and searching.

As the woman advanced slowly toward her, Dianthe was conscious of a thrill of fear, which quickly passed as she dimly remembered having heard the servants jesting over old Aunt Hannah, the most noted "voodoo" doctor or witch in the country.

"Come in honey, and res'," were her first words after her keen eyes had traveled over the woman before her. Dianthe obeyed without a murmur; in truth, she seemed again to have lost her own will in another's.

The one-roomed cabin was faultlessly neat, and the tired girl was grateful for the warmth of the glowing brands upon the wide hearth. Very soon a cup of stimulating coffee warmed her tired frame and brought more animation to her tired face.

"What may your name be, Auntie?" she asked at length, uneasy at the furtive glances cast by the eyes of the silent figure seated in the distant shadow of the chimney-corner. The eyes never wavered, but no answer was vouchsafed her by the woman in the corner. Somewhere she had read a description of an African princess which fitted the woman before her.

> "I knew a princess; she was old,
>   Crisp-haired, flat-featured, with a look
> Such as no dainty pen of gold
>   Would write of in a fairy book.
>
> "Her face was like a Sphinx's face, to me,
>   Touched with a vast patience, desert grace,
> And lonesome, brooding mystery."

Suddenly a low sound, growing gradually louder, fell upon Dianthe's ear; it was the voice of the old woman crooning a mournful minor cadence, but for an instant it sent a chill about the girl's heart. It was a funeral chant commonly sung by the Negroes over the dead. It chimed in with her gloomy, despairing mood and startled her. She arose hastily to her feet to leave the place.

"How can I reach the road to Livingston Place?" she asked with a shudder of apprehension as she glanced at her entertainer.

"Don't be 'feared, child; Aunt Hannah won't hurt a ha'r of that purty head. Hain't it these arms done nussed ev'ry Livingston? I knowed your mother, child; for all you're married to Marse Aubrey, you isn't a white 'ooman."

"I do not deny what you say, Auntie; I have no desire so to do," replied Dianthe gently.

With a cry of anguish the floodgates of feeling were unloosed, and the old Negress flung her arms about the delicate form. "Gawd-a-mercy! My Mira's gal! My Mira's gal!" Then followed a harrowing scene.

Dianthe listened to the old story of sowing the wind and reaping the whirlwind. A horrible, paralyzing dread was upon her. Was she never to cease from suffering and be at rest? Rocking herself to and fro, and moaning as though in physical pain, the old woman told her story.

"I was born on de Livingston place, an' bein' a purty likely gal, was taken to de big house when I was a tot. I was trained by ol' Miss'. As soon as I was growed up, my mistress changed in her treatment of me, for she soon knowed of my relations with massa, an' she was hurt to de heart, po' 'ooman. Mira was de onlies' child of ten that my massa lef' me for my comfort; all de res' were sold away to raise de mor'gage off de prop'rty.

"Ol' marse had only one chil', a son; he was eddicated for a doctor, and of all the limb o' de devil, he was de worst. After ol' marse an' ol' miss' was dead he took a shine to Mira, and for years he stuck to her in great shape. Her fust chil was Reuel—"

"What!" shrieked Dianthe. "Tell me—quick, for God's sake! Is he alive, and by what name is he known?" She was deathly white, and spread out her hands as if seeking support.

"Yes, he's living, or was a year ago. He's called Dr. Reuel Briggs, an' many a dollar he has sent his ol' granny, may the good Marster bless him!"

"Tell me all—tell me the rest," came from the lips of the trembling girl.

"Her second child was a girl,—a beautiful, delicate child, an' de Doctor fairly worshipped her. Dat leetle gal was yourself, an' I'm your granny."

"Then Reuel Briggs is my brother!"

"Certain; but let me tell you the res', honey. Dese things jes' got to happen in slavery, but I isn't gwine to wink at de debbil's wurk wif both eyes open. An' I doesn't want you to keep on livin' with Marse Aubrey Livingston. It's too wicked; it's flyin' in de face ob Almighty God. I'se wanted to tell you eber sense I knowed who he'd married. After a while de Doctor got to thinkin' 'bout keepin' up de family name, an' de fus' thing we knows he up an' marries a white lady down to Charleston, an' brings her home. Well! when she found out all de family secrets she made de house too hot to hol' Mira, and it was ordered that she mus' be sold away. I got on my knees to marse an' I prayed to him not to do it, but to give Mira a house on de place where she could be alone an' bring up de childrun, an' he would a done it but for his wife."

The old woman paused to moan and rock and weep over the sad memories of the past. Dianthe sat like a stone woman.

"Den I believe de debbil took possession of me body and soul. A week before my po' gal was to be sol', Misses' child was born, and died in about an hour; at about de same time Mira gave birth to a son, too. In de 'citemen' de idea come to me to change de babies, fer no one would know it, I being alone when de chil' died, an' de house wil' fer fear misses would die. So I changed de babies, an' tol' Marse Livingston dat Mira's boy was de dead one. So, honey, Aubrey is your own blood brother an' you got to quit dat house mejuntly."

"My brother!"

Dianthe stood over the old woman and shook her by the arm, with a look of utter horror that froze her blood. "My brothers! both those men!"

The old woman mumbled and groaned, then started up.

Aunt Hannah breathed hard once or twice. Minute after minute passed. From time to time she glanced at Dianthe, her hard, toil-worn hands strained at the arms of her chair as if to break them. Her mind seemed wavering as she crooned:

"My Mira's children, by de lotus-lily on each leetle breast I claim them for de great Osiris, mighty god. Honey, hain't you a flower on yur breast?"

Dianthe bowed her head in assent, for speech had deserted her. Then old Aunt Hannah undid her snowy kerchief and her dress, and displayed to the terrified girl the perfect semblance of a lily cut, as it were, in shining ebony.

"Did each of Mira's children have this mark?"

"Yes, honey; all of one blood!"

Dianthe staggered as though buffeted in the face. Blindly, as if in some hideous trance, reeling and stumbling, she fell. Cold and white as marble, she lay in the old woman's arms, who thought her dead. "Better so," she cried, and then laughed aloud, then kissed the poor, drawn face. But she was not dead.

Time passed; the girl could not speak. The sacrilege of what had been done was too horrible. Such havoc is wrought by evil deeds. The first downward step of an individual or a nation, who can tell where it will end, through what dark and doleful shades of hell the soul must pass in travail?

> *"The laws of changeless justice bind*
> *Opressor and oppressed;*
> *And close as sin and suffering joined,*
> *We march to Fate abreast."*

The slogan of the hour is "Keep the Negro down!" but who is clear enough in vision to decide who hath black blood and who hath it not? Can any one tell? No, not one; for in His own mysterious way He has united the white race and the black race in this new continent. By the transgression of the law He proves His own infallibility: "Of one blood have I made all nations of men to dwell upon the whole face of the earth," is as true today as when given to the inspired writers to be recorded. No man can draw the dividing line between the two races, for they are both of one blood!

Bending a little, as though very weak, and leaning heavily upon her old grandmother's arm, Dianthe at length set out for the Hall. Her face was lined and old with suffering. All hope was gone; despair was heavy on her young shoulders whose life was blasted in its bloom by the passions of others.

As she looked upward at the grey, leaden sky, tears slowly trickled down her cheeks. "God have mercy!" she whispered.

CHAPTER XXII

OR two days Mrs. Livingston brooded in her chamber. Fifty times a day Aubrey asked for her. The maid told him she was ill, but not alarmingly so; no physician was called. She was simply indisposed, could not be seen.

Gazing in Dianthe's face, the maid whispered, "She sleeps. I will not disturb her."

Alone, she springs from her couch with all the energy of life and health. She paced the room. For two long hours she never ceased her dreary walk. Memories crowded around her, wreathing themselves in shapes which floated mistily through her brain. Her humble school days at Fisk; her little heart leaping at the well-won prize; the merry play with her joyous mates; in later years, the first triumphant throb when wondering critics praised the melting voice, and world-admiring crowds applauded. And, O, the glorious days of travel in Rome and Florence! the classic scenes of study; intimate companionship with Beethoven, Mozart and Hayden; the floods of inspiration poured in strains of self-made melody upon her soul. Then had followed the reaction, the fall into unscrupulous hands, and the ruin that had come upon her innocent head.

The third day Mrs. Livingston arose, dressed, and declaring herself quite well, went to walk. She returned late in the afternoon, dined with her husband, conversed and even laughed. After dinner they walked a while upon the broad piazzas, beneath the silent stars and gracious moon, inhaling the cold, bracing air. Then Aubrey begged her for a song. Once again she sang "Go down, Moses," and all the house was hushed to drink in the melody of that exquisite voice.

To mortal eyes, this young pair and their surroundings marked them as darlings of the gods enjoying the world's heaped-up felicity. Could these same eyes have looked deeper into their hearts, not the loathsome cell of the wretch condemned to death could have shown a sight more hideous. 'Twas late. Pausing at her chamber door, Aubrey raised her hand to his lips with courtly grace, and bade her good-night.

* * * * *

It was the first hours of the morning. From the deepest and most dreamless slumber that had ever sealed his eyes, Aubrey awoke just as the clock was striking two. 'Twas quite dark, and at first he felt that the striking clock had awakened him; yet sleep on the instant was as effectually banished from his eyes as if it were broad daylight. He could not distinguish the actual contact of any substance, and yet he could not rid himself of the feeling that a strong arm was holding him forcibly down, and a heavy hand was on his lips. He saw nothing, though the moon's rays shone full into the room. He felt nothing sensuously, but everything sensationally; and thus it was that with eyes half-closed, and seemingly fixed as by an iron vice, he beheld the door of his dressing-room—the private means of communication with Dianthe's rooms—very cautiously opened, and Dianthe herself, in a loose robe, crept into the room, and stealthily as a spirit glide to the side of his bed.

Arrested by the same trance-like yet conscious power that bound his form but left perception free, Aubrey neither spoke nor moved. And yet he felt, and partially beheld her stoop over him, listen to his breathing, pass her hand before his eyes to try if they would open; then he, with sidelong glance, beheld her, rapidly as thought, take up the night glass standing on his table, and for the glass containing clear cold water, which it was his custom to swallow every morning upon first awakening, substitute one which, he had seen from the first, she carried in her hand. This done, the stealthy figure moved away, gently drew back the door, and would have passed; but no—the spell was broken. A hand was on her shoulder—a hand of iron. Back it dragged her— into the room just left, shut the door and locked it, held her in its sinewy strength till other doors were locked, then bore her to the bed, placed her upon it, and then released her. And there she sat, white and silent as the grave, whilst before her stood Aubrey, pale as herself, but no longer silent.

Taking the glass which she had substituted, he held it to her lips, and pronounced one word— "Drink!" But one word; but O, what a world of destiny, despair, and agony hung on that word; again and again repeated. Her wild and haggard eyes, her white, speechless lips, all, alas! bore testimony to her guilt—to a mind unbalanced, but only added determination to Aubrey's deep, unflinching purpose.

"Drink! deeper yet! Pledge me to the last drop; drink deep; drink all!"

"Aubrey, Aubrey! mercy, as you look for it! let me explain—" The shrinking woman was on her knees, the half-drained glass in her hand.

"Drink!" shouted Aubrey. "Drain the glass to Reuel!"

"To Reuel!" gasped Dianthe, and set the glass down empty. Once more Aubrey led his bride of three months back to the door of her room. Once more before her chamber door he paused; and once again, but now in mockery, he stooped and kissed her hand.

"Farewell, my love," he said. "When we meet, 'twill be—"

"In judgment, Aubrey; and may God have mercy on our guilty souls!"

CHAPTER XXIII

 WAS a cold gray morning; the dawn of such a day as seems to wrap itself within the shroud of night, hiding the warm sun in its stony bosom, and to creep through time arrayed in mourning garments for the departed stars. Aubrey was up by the earliest glimpse of dawn. Uncertain what to do or where to go, he made a pretence of eating, sitting in solemn state in the lonely breakfast room, where the servants glided about in ghostly silence, which was too suggestive for the overwrought nerves of the master of all that magnificence. Fifty times he asked the maid for Mrs. Livingston. The woman told him she was ill,—not alarmingly so; no physician's services were needed, neither his own nor another's. He did not ask to see her, yet with a strange and morbid curiosity, he kept on questioning how she was, and why she kept her chamber, until the knowing laugh and sly joke about the anxiety of bridegrooms over the welfare of brides made the servants' quarters ring with hilarity. At length, tired of his aimless wandering, he said he'd go. His valet asked him where. He could not tell. "Pack up some things."

"For how long a time, sir?"

"I cannot tell, James."

"Shall I order the carriage?"

"Anything, something! A horse; yes. I'll have the swiftest one in the stable. A valise—no more; no, you need not come. I must be alone."

In Dianthe's room the attendants tread noiselessly, and finally leave her to enjoy her feigned slumber. She waits but the closing of the door, to spring from her couch with all the seeming energy of life and health. First she went to the window and flung wide the hangings, letting in a flood of light upon the pale, worn face reflected in the mirror. What a wondrous change was there! The long white drapery of her morning robe fell about her like a shroud, yet, white as it was, contrasted painfully with the livid ash-hue of her skin. Her arms were thin and blue, her hands transparent; her sunny hair hung in long disheveled, waving masses, the picture of neglect; the sunken, wan brow, and livid lips, the heavy eyes with deep, black halos round them—all these made up a ruined temple.

"When he comes he will not know me," she murmured to herself; then sighing deeply, turned and paced the room. What she thought of, none could say. She spoke not; never raised her eyes from off the ground, nor ceased her dreary walk for two long hours. She sometimes sobbed, but never shed a tear.

Here we drop the veil. Let no human eye behold the writhings of that suffering face, the torture of that soul unmoored, and cast upon the sea of wildest passion, without the pilot, principle, or captain of all salvation, God, to trust in,— passion, adoration of a human idol, hereditary traits entirely unbalanced, generous, but fervid impulses, her only guides. She knew that her spiritual person must survive the grave, but what that world was where her spirit was fast tending, only the dread tales of fear and superstition shadowed truth; and now, when her footsteps were pressing to it, horror and dread dogged every footprint.

Hour after hour elapsed alone. O, 'twas agony to be alone! She could not bear it. She would call her maid; but no, her cold, unimpassioned face would bring no comfort to her aching heart, aching for pity, for some cheering bosom, where she might sob her ebbing life away. The door opens,—and O joy! old Aunt Hannah's arms enfold her. For hours the two sat in solemn conference, while the servants wondered and speculated over the presence of the old witch.

At last night fell. "Mother," murmured the dying girl, raising her head from off her damp pillow. "A very golden cloud is printed with the fleecy words of glory. 'I will return.'" She pointed to the golden clouds banking the western sky. "O, will our spirits come, like setting suns, on each tomorrow of eternity?"

For answer, the old woman raised her hand in warning gesture. There sounded distinct and clear—three loud, yet muffled knocks on the panel directly above the couch where Dianthe lay.

"'Tis nothing, mother; I'm used to it now," said the girl with indifference.

"You say 'tis nuffin, honey; but yer limbs are quiverin' wif pain, and the drops ob agony is on yer po' white face. You can't 'ceive me, chile; yer granny knows de whole circumstance. I seed it all las' night in my dreams. Vengeance is mine; I will repay. One comes who is de instrumen' ob de Lord." And the old woman muttered and rocked and whispered.

Whatever was the cause of Mrs. Livingston's illness, its character was unusual and alarming. The maid, who was really attached to the beautiful bride, pleaded to be allowed to send for medical aid in vain. The causes for her suffering, as stated by Dianthe, were plausible; but her resolve to have no aid, inflexible. As evening advanced, her restlessness, and the hideous action of spasmodic pains across her livid face, became distressing. To all the urgent appeals of her servants, she simply replied she was waiting for some one. He was coming soon—very soon and then she would be quite well.

And yet he came not. From couch to door, from door to window; with eager, listening ear and wistful eyes the poor watcher traversed her chamber in unavailing expectancy. At length a sudden calm seemed to steal over her; the incessant restlessness of her wearied frame yielded to a tranquil, passive air. She lay upon cushions piled high upon the couch commanding a view of the broad hallways leading to her apartments. The beams of the newly risen moon bathed every object in the dim halls. Clear as the vesper bell, sounding across a far distant lake, strains of delicious music, rising and falling in alternate cadence of strong martial measure, came floating in waves of sound down the corridor.

Dianthe and Aunt Hannah and the maid heard the glorious echoes; whilst in the town the villagers heard the music as of a mighty host. Louder it grew, first in low and wailing notes, then swelling, pealing through arch and corridor in mighty diapason, until the very notes of different instruments rang out as from a vast orchestra. There was the thunder of the organ, the wild harp's peal, the aeolian's sigh, the trumpet's peal, and the mournful horn. A thousand soft melodious flutes, like trickling streams upheld a bird-like treble; whilst ever and anon the muffled drum with awful beat precise, the rolling kettle and the crashing cymbals, kept time to sounds like tramping of a vast but viewless army. Nearer they came. The dull, deep beat of falling feet—in the hall—up the stairs. Louder it came and louder. Louder and yet more loud the music swelled to thunder! The unseen mass must have been the disembodied souls of every age since Time began, so vast the rush and strong the footfalls. And then the chant of thousands of voices swelling in rich, majestic choral tones, joined in the thundering crash. It was the welcome of ancient Ethiopia to her dying daughter of the royal line.

Upspringing from her couch, as through the air the mighty hallelujah sounded, Dianthe with frantic gestures and wild distended eyes, cried: "I see them now! the glorious band! Welcome, great masters of the world's first birth! All hail, my royal ancestors—Candace, Semiramis, Dido, Solomon, David and the great kings of early days, and the great masters of the world of song. O, what long array of souls divine, lit with immortal fire from heaven itself! O, let me kneel to thee! And to thee, too, Beethoven, Mozart, thou sons of song! Divine ones, art thou come to take me home? Me, thy poor worshipper on earth? O, let me be thy child in paradise!

The pageant passed, or seemed to pass, from her whose eyes alone of all the awe-struck listeners, with mortal gaze beheld them. When, at length, the last vibrating echoes of the music seemed to die away in utter vacant silence to the terrified attendants, Dianthe still seemed to listen. Either her ear still drank in the music, or another sound had caught her attention.

"Hark, hark! 'Tis carriage wheels. Do you not hear them? Now they pass the railroad at the crossing. Hasten, O hasten! Still they have a long mile to traverse. O, hasten! They call me home."

For many minutes she sat rigid and cold as marble. The trembling maid wept in silent terror and grief, for the gentle bride was a kind mistress. Old Aunt Hannah, with a fortitude born of despair, ministered in every possible way to the dying girl. To the great relief of all, at last, there came to their ears the very distant rumbling of wheels. Nearer it came—it sounded in the avenue—it paused at the great entrance, some one alighted—a stir—the sound of voices—then footsteps—the ascent of footsteps on the stairs. Nearer, nearer yet; hastily they come, like messengers of speed. They're upon the threshold—enter. Then, and not till then, the rigid lady moved. With one wild scream of joy she rushed forward, and Reuel Briggs clasped her in his arms.

For a few brief moments, the wretched girl lived an age in

heaven. The presence of that one beloved—this drop of joy sweetened all the bitter draught and made for her an eternity of compensation. With fond wild tenderness she gazed upon him, gazed in his anxious eyes until her own looked in his very soul, and stamped there all the story of her guilt and remorse. Then winding her cold arms around his neck, she laid her weary head upon his shoulder and silently as the night passed through the portals of the land of souls.

CHAPTER XXIV

WAS midnight. The landscape was still as death. Hills, rocks, rivers, even the babbling brooks, seemed locked in sleep. The moonbeams dreamt upon the hillside; stars slept in the glittering sky; the silent vales were full of dreaming flowers whose parti-colored cups closed in sleep. In all that solemn hush of silence one watcher broke the charmed spell. 'Twas Aubrey Livingston. Now he moves swiftly over the plain as if some sudden purpose drove him on; then he turns back in the self-same track and with the same impulsive speed. What is he doing in the lonely night? All day, hour after hour, mile on mile, the scorching midday sun had blazed upon his head, and still he wandered on. The tranquil sunset purpled round his way and still the wanderer hastened on. In his haggard eyes one question seems to linger—"I wonder if she lives!"

Many, many dreary times he said this question over! He has a secret and 'tis a mighty one; he fears if human eye but look upon him, it must be revealed. Hark! suddenly there falls upon his ear the sound of voices, surely some one called! Again! His straining ear caught a familiar sound.

"Aubrey! Aubrey Livingston!"

"By heaven, it is her voice!" he told himself. And as if to assure him still more of who addressed him, close before his very eyes moved two figures. Hand in hand they passed from out a clump of sheltering trees, and slowly crossed his path. One face was turned toward him, the other from him. The moon revealed the same white robe in which he had last beheld her, the long, streaming hair, her slippered feet—all were there. Upon his wondering eyes her own were fixed in mute appeal and deepest anguish; then both figures passed away, he knew not where.

"'Twas she, and in full life. God of heaven, she lives!"

Pausing not to think he was deceived, enough for him, she lived. He turned his steps toward his home, with flying feet he neared the hall. Just as he reached the great entrance gates, he saw the two figures lightly in advance of him. This time Dianthe's face was turned away, but the silver moonbeams threw into bold relief the accusing face of Molly Vance!

With a sudden chill foreboding, he entered the hall and passed up the stairs to his wife's apartments. He opened wide the door and stood within the chamber of the dead.

There lay the peaceful form—spread with a drapery of soft, white gauze around her, and only the sad and livid, poisoned face was visible above it; and kneeling by the side of her, his first love and his last—was Reuel Briggs.

Rising from the shadows as Aubrey entered, Charlie Vance, flanked on either side by Ai and Abdadis, moved to meet him, the stern brow and sterner words of an outraged brother and friend greeted him:

"Welcome, murderer!"

*　*　*　*　*

Dianthe was dead, poisoned; that was clear. Molly Vance was unduly done to death by the foul treachery of the same hand. All this was now clear to the thinking public, for so secluded had Aubrey Livingston lived since his return to the United States, that many of his intimate associates still believed that he had perished in the accident on the Charles. It was quite evident to these friends that his infatuation for the beautiful Dianthe had led to the commission of a crime. But the old adage that, "the dead tell no tales," was not to be set aside for visionary ravings unsupported by lawful testimony.

Livingston's wealth purchased shrewd and active lawyers to defend him against the charges brought by the Vances—father and son,—and Reuel Briggs.

One interview which was never revealed to public comment, took place between Ai, Abdadis, Aunt Hannah, Reuel Briggs and Aubrey Livingston.

Aubrey sat alone in his sumptuous study. An open book was on his knees, but his eyes were fixed on vacancy. He was changed and his auburn locks were prematurely grey. His eyes revealed an impenetrable mystery within into whose secret depths no mortal eye might look. Thus he sat when the group we have named above silently surrounded him. "Peace, O son of Osiris, to thy parting hour!"

Thus Ai greeted him. There was no mistaking these words, and gazing into the stern faces of the silent group Aubrey knew that something of import was about to happen.

Aubrey did not change countenance, although he glanced at Reuel as if seeking mercy. The latter did not change countenance; only his eyes, those strange deep eyes before whose fixed gaze none could stand unflinching, took on a more sombre glow. Again Ai spoke:

"God has willed it! Great is the God of Ergamenes, we are but worms beneath His feet. His will be done." Then began a strange, weird scene. Round and round the chair where Aubrey was seated walked the kingly Ai chanting in a low, monotone in his native tongue, finally advancing with measured steps to a position directly opposite and facing Livingston, and stood there erect and immovable, with arms raised as if in invocation. His eyes glittered with strange, fascinating lights in the shaded room. To the man seated there it seemed that an eternity was passing. Why did not these two men he had injured take human vengeance in meting out punishment to him? And why, oh! why did those eyes, piercing his own like poinards, hold him so subtly in their spell?

Gradually he yielded to the mysterious beatitude that in sensibly enwrapped his being. Detached from terrestrial bonds his spirit soared in regions of pure ethereal blue. A delicious torpor held him in its embrace. His head sank upon his breast. His eyes closed in a trancelike slumber.

Ai quitted his position, and approaching Aubrey, lifted one of the shut eyelids. "He sleeps!" he exclaimed.

Then standing by the side of the unconscious man he poured into his ear—speaking loudly and distinctly,—a few terse sentences. Not a muscle moved in the faces of those standing about the sleeper. Then Ai passed his hands lightly over his face, made a few upward passes, and turning to his companions, beckoned them to follow him from the room. Silently as they had come the group left the house and grounds, gained a waiting carriage and were driven rapidly away. In the shelter of the vehicle Charlie Vance spoke, "Is justice done?" he sternly queried.

"Justice will be done," replied Ai's soothing tones.

"Then I am satisfied."

But Reuel spoke not one word.

*   *   *   *   *

One day not very long after this happening, the body of Aubrey Livingston was found floating in the Charles river at the very point where poor Molly Vance had floated in the tangled lily-bed. The mysterious command of Ai, "death by thine own hand," whispered in his ear while under hypnotic influence, had been followed to the last letter.

Thus Aubrey had become his own executioner according to the ancient laws of the inhabitants of Telassar. Members of the royal family in direct line to the throne became their own executioners when guilty of the crime of murder.

*   *   *   *   *

Reuel Briggs returned to the Hidden City with his faithful subjects, and old Aunt Hannah. There he spends his days in teaching his people all that he has learned in years of contact with modern culture. United to Candace, his days glide peacefully by in good works; but the shadows of great sins darken his life, and the memory of past joys is ever with him. He views, too, with serious apprehension, the advance of mighty nations penetrating the dark, mysterious forests of his native land.

"Where will it stop?" he sadly questions. "What will the end be?"

But none save Omnipotence can solve the problem.

To our human intelligence these truths depicted in this feeble work may seem terrible,—even horrible. But who shall judge the handiwork of God, the Great Craftsman! Caste prejudice, race pride, boundless wealth, scintillating intellects refined by all the arts of the intellectual world, are but puppets in His hand, for His promises stand, and He will prove His words, "Of one blood have I made all races of men."

THE END.

EPILOGUE

The Givens Foundation for African-American Literature

YOU HAVE to know where you came from to understand where you are going. This familiar expression of the value of history is at the heart of the Givens Foundation for African-American Literature. Our mission is to promote historical and contemporary black literature. This partnership with Washington Square Press to republish out-of-print African-American classics helps accomplish the goal of keeping literature and its lessons alive.

The Givens Foundation is inspired by and draws its mission from the Archie Givens, Sr. Collection of African-American Literature. Housed at the University of Minnesota's Elmer L. Andersen Library, the Collection includes over 9,000 books, pamphlets, manuscripts, letters and ephemera representing more than two centuries of African-American cultural accomplishment. Many of these items are signed, rare, and first edition volumes. Each year hundreds of books, ranging from novels, plays, poems, short stories, and autobiographies, to nonfiction and scholarly titles, join the collection and enhance its portrayal of the African-American experience.

While we protect these historical artifacts for future generations in a secure environment, we also strive to keep their content circulating, so that contemporary audiences can learn from their timeless messages. The Givens Foundation actively celebrates and promotes African-American literature and history. Our public programs, readings, conferences and exhibits build on the collection and increase public awareness of African-American writers. Using themes such as the Harlem Renaissance and the Black Arts Movement, we also create online lesson plans and teacher-training seminars for educators seeking African-American literary resources for the classroom.

The Givens Collection Classics series is an exciting new venture because it unveils powerful stories and expressions from over a century ago. We believe that our past informs and shapes both our present and future. And it is our profound hope that a new generation of readers will discover these books, gain a deeper understanding of our multifaceted American history, and an increased ability to appreciate the texture of the lives that lie ahead of us.

>*—Archie Givens, Jr.*
>*President*
>*Givens Foundation for*
>*African-American Literature*